The Return of a Japanese Private Medic from Luzon Island

陸軍衛生二等兵 ルソン島生還記

昭和18年暮れ、ルソン島の１３９兵站病院ムニオス分院勤務となった陸軍衛生二等兵が体験した苛烈なる戦場。
敗走する日本軍を襲う米軍機、砲弾の雨、ゲリラ、飢餓、マラリアなど、地獄の戦場から九死に一生を得て生還した男の体験手記！

At the end of 1943, a Private medical soldier worked in the 139th Logistics branch hospital in Muñoz of Luzon Island. He had experienced a fierce battlefield. U.S. planes, a rain of shells, guerrillas, starvation, and malaria attacked the retreating Japanese forces.
This is the memoir of a man who barely escaped death on the hell battlefield.

濱辺 政雄
Hamabe Masao

目　　次

（注意）本の左のページは日本語、右のページは対訳された英語となっております。

TABLE OF CONTENTS

Note

The English on the right page is an English translation of the Japanese on the left page.

陸軍衛生二等兵 濱辺政雄

出征、終戦、復員

餓死寸前の地獄の底より這い登るようにして復員、故郷の土を踏んで40年余の歳月が流れ去り、妻をめとり、子が出来、孫が出来、私も64才の誕生日を迎える歳になりました。

40年の歳月に流されるかの様に比島派遣軍威九七六七部隊（第百三十九兵站病院）での数々の想い出も忘れ去り、日々の生活の中に埋没してしまっています。年に一度の一三九会にも出席出来ない毎年です。会の開催の通知がくる度に今年は今年はと思っています。

何回か出席した戦友会で想い出す事は、ムニオス時代の同年兵、同じ内務班同じ病室勤務で共にビンタの洗礼を受け共に涙を流したり笑ったり、貴様と俺と言い合った友の顔が見えない事が一抹のさみしさを感じます。

皆それぞれ筆舌ではあらわせられない苦しみの中で食糧の不足とマラリア、アメーバ赤痢におかされ、日本軍の勝利と内地故郷の肉親を想いつつ、アシン河の河原に草むしてやがて白骨となり消滅して行った事でしょう。今日まで生を受け子供等や孫等にかこまれての日々、亡き戦友のお蔭と感謝しています。私のつたない筆にたくして「想い出の記」を書き在天の戦友の霊に捧げたいと思います。

（昭和61年新春、記す）

Masao Hamabe, the Private Medic in Japan Army,
to the front, then the end of war and demobilization

written by Masao Hamabe

translated by Junichi Hamabe

I was demobilized as if I had crawled up from an abyss of hell where I was on the verge of starvation. It has been over forty years since I returned to my hometown. I got married and had children and grandchildren. This year, 1986, I will be 64 years old.

My memories of the 139th Logistics Hospital in the Philippines are fading in forty years of daily life. How I wish I could attend the 139th Corps reunion. I decided in vain to go the next time I received the invitation.

At the reunions I attended several times, I remembered my fellow soldiers in Muñoz. I worked with them in the same hospital and internal affairs corps, shedding tears or laughing, given a slap across the face. It is sad when I realize I can't see some of them.

Those people must have suffered from starvation, malaria, and amoebic dysentery. Their distress was beyond description. Thinking about family in the homeland or believing in Japan's victory, they died on the Asin riverside. They were covered with weed, reduced to bleached bones, then disappeared.

I am grateful to the deceased fellow soldiers for my days with children and grandchildren.

I have described my recollections to dedicate to the souls in heaven.

Described in early spring 1986

1　出征

昭和17年　兵隊検査第二乙種合格。

昭和18年9月20日、西部第四十七部隊に入隊。

その頃私の村でも私と同じ年頃の若者は召集でいなくなり、私など最後の方で、いらいらしていましたので、なんとなくほっとした感じでした。

10月初め頃、南方方面部隊に転属と言う事で私達中隊の同年兵が半分くらい指名され、私もその中の一人でした。大陸方面より南の方が良いだろうと思って嬉しく感じました。

入隊以来、起床ラッパに起こされ、消灯ラッパの鳴るまで毎日毎日、初年兵教育を受け軍人精神をたたき込まれること1ヵ月。

10月20日大村駅より乗車、小倉駅下車。小倉陸軍病院まで歩く途中の街角で、おばあさんが私達の方に向き手を合わせ、「御苦労様です」とおがんでいた。これ以上修理出来ないと思われるよれよれの軍服、軍靴、帽子をかぶり、日にやけた顔は真っ黒、戦地帰りの兵隊と思っているのではないかと。なんとなく恥ずかしくなった。

誰かが、「自分達の身に着けている物は、もう二度と使用されそうもない物ばかりで50人分の被服をまた持って帰るのは大変だから、小倉に着いて着替を支給されたら焼却するのだ」と、わかったようなことを言っていた。

引率者は陸軍伍長一人、編成が出来上がるまで何もする事がなく毎日のんびりしていた。しばらく過ぎて、上等兵、伍長、軍曹など

1 To the front as a medical soldier

1942 January	The draft test to Class B+
1943 September 20	Drafted into the Western 47th Corps

Many young men in my village had been drafted, so I felt somewhat relieved when I received a draft card.

At the beginning of October, half of my fellow soldiers in the company were to be transferred to the southern army corps. My name was among them. I felt it better to go to the south than to China. We received recruit training and warrior spirit every day from reveille to taps for a month.

October 20, we got on the train at Omura and got off at Kokura. At the street corner on the way to Kokura Army Hospital, I saw an old woman praying for us with her palms joined. "Thank you, soldiers, for all you have done for us," she said. She might have thought we were soldiers from the battlefield. We were tanned, with worn-out uniforms, shoes, and caps that appeared unable to mend. I got somewhat embarrassed.

Somebody said knowingly, "Things we wear aren't likely to be used. It's hard to bring back fifty people's clothes. So they'll burn them at Kokura once they distribute new ones."

There was only one leader, Corporal. We spent calm days waiting for the formation announcement. Soon, private first class (PFC), corporals, and sergeants joined our army every day.

と毎日の様に入営して来た。娑婆の気持がぬけない様で、地方の言葉で私達に話しかけたりしていた。

やがて部隊の編成も整い、11月5日、小倉の北方練兵場で出陣式を挙げる。

下着から軍服軍靴、何もかも身にぴったり合った新品の服をまとったピカピカの初年兵だった。小倉より門司港まで完全軍装で行軍した。沿道には多くの人が万歳をさけび私達を見送ってくれた。一生懸命やらねばいかんと思い行軍した。夏服なので11月初冬の門司港は寒かった。

やがて乗船出港。船の上甲板と二番甲板の間に木材で中二階に仕切を設けていた。立ち上がることの出来ない高さで小さくなっていた。明け方、済州島沖にさしかかった時、潜水艦の警報が鳴り、急いで救命袋を身にまとい甲板よりさげている縄梯子をよじ登る途中、2発目の爆発音が聞こえた。甲板に登り海を見たら私達の横を走っていた船がやられたらしい。船首を垂直に立て、ヅボッと沈む姿が一瞬目に入り、身がしまり足がガクガクふるえた。30隻の船団は隊形をくずし各船全速で走り出した。

私達が乗った船は大分古く速力も6ノットしか出ないと言うことで見る見る僚船に取り残されて心細く、護衛艦は二隻、海防艦が何百トン位か、小さい艦が右往左往しながら爆雷を落としている。波と波の間に見え隠れしていて波にのまれそうで心配だ。

They seemed not to get out of the feeling of everyday life yet. So they behaved like ordinary people and talked to us in their local dialect.

Before long, the military unit formation was ready. On November 5, a kickoff ceremony was held at Kitagata Drill Court in Kokura. We were shiny recruits with new clothes that fit from underwear to uniforms and shoes. We marched from Kokura to Moji Port, fully armed. Many people saw us off along the street, shouting, "Banzai!".

I marched, thinking I must do whatever I could for them. We wore summer uniforms, so I felt cold at Moji Port in November early winter.

Soon, we boarded and departed. Our space was between the upper and second decks, separated by a wooden plate to make one more floor. The height was insufficient for standing.

Early the following day, an alarm for a submarine rang. We put on our life jackets in a hurry and went up the rope ladder. Then we heard a second explosion. The ship beside us had been attacked. Climbing up the deck, I saw the ship's bow rise and sink vertically for a moment. I felt my legs trembling. The convoy of 30 ships broke down the formation and began to run by each at full speed.

Our ship was old and made 6 knots at most. We felt uneasy that we were left alone. Two small escort ships were moving around in confusion and dropping depth bombs. I was worried that our ship, tossed by the waves, would be swallowed up.

前途多難をふと感じて薄ら寒くなる。やがて警報が解除され、船室に入る。その後潜水艦の情報は入っている様だったが、私達はなんとなくのんびりと日を送っていた。

だんだん暑くなり出した。船酔い患者が出て来て、私の班でもほとんどが酔い、ゲーゲー、青い顔をして苦しみ、飯など喉を通らない。私と同年兵の永野君と2人だけは、船酔にならず航海中は飯を腹一杯食べられて嬉しかった。船酔が良くなると皆の食欲も出て来て、少ない飯が気に入らず、海が荒れてまた皆船酔いになれば良いと悪いことを考えたり話し合ったりしていた。

11月18日、台湾の高雄港に投錨、約10日滞在。

毎日酒保品としてバナナが一房配給された。その頃日本内地ではなかなか口に入らない果物で、皆、夢中になって食べ、何日か目には、とうとう下痢になってしまった。船内に寝ていたのでは便所が遠いので、便所の近くに寝ていた。悪い奴は便所の屋根の上に寝ていた。甲板の上に仮の便所が数ヵ所造られていた。

毎日暑い日が続き、日中は甲板に出て日陰をさがして戦友同士想い想いの話に花を咲かせていた。

I Suddenly felt many difficulties ahead, and I got a slight chill. After a while, the warning was called off, and we returned to the cabin. After that, there was some information about submarines. But we spent days relaxing.

It was getting hotter. Many soldiers got seasick. Being pale, they vomited. They could barely eat. However, one of my fellow soldiers, Mr. Nagano, and I did not get seasick, and we were happy eating as much food as possible.

Soon, they recovered from their seasickness and had an appetite. There would be less food for Mr. Nagano and me. A wicked idea occurred to Nagano and me. We wished the sea would be rough and they would suffer from seasickness again.

We anchored at Takao Port in Taiwan on November 18 and stayed there for ten days. A bunch of bananas was distributed every day. Bananas were rare in our homeland, so we devoured them until a few days later we had diarrhea.

I slept near the restroom because our cabin was a long way from there. The shrewd guys were resting on the roof of the lavatory. Several temporary toilets had been built on the deck.

Hot days continued every day. We gathered in the shade on the deck during the day and had a good time chatting.

2　マニラ　ムニオス

12 月 4 日未明マニラ港に入港、装具を身に着けて待機。岸壁を通る比島人を見ると、皆原色のシャツやズボンを着用しているので、洋画を見ている様な感じだった。

11 時下船、夕方近く兵站宿舎に入る。途すがら比島の子供達が愛国行進曲など日本の軍歌を日本語で上手に歌っているのを聞いて感心し、「友達、友達」と近寄り煙草をもらったりしているのに驚いた。

一度飛行場建設の使役に行った。初めてマニラの市街をトラックに乗って飛行場までの往復で、見なれない南国の家並、人々の服装など物めずらしく、また、「バンザイ、バンザイ」と日本語で手を上げ連呼しているのにも驚く。ビックリする事ばかり。

12 月 12 日、１３９兵站病院開設。

私はムニオス分院（原田隊）要員だった。

患者を収容治療に当たる事になり、マニラ駅より汽車に乗り、ムニオスに向かう。明治時代の汽車のような、小さな機関車が小さな客車を四輌位引いてボーポーポと走り出した。比島人も一緒に乗込んでいたようだった。屋根の上にもお客が乗っていて、盛んに奇声を発し楽しそうに話し合っていた。途中で突然汽車が停まった。「なんだろう？」「さあ、なんだろうかね。ちょっと見てくる」と同年兵の○○君が機関車の方に行った。

2 Manila and Muñoz

Our ship entered Manila Port early in the morning of December 4. We stood by on the ship, armed. I saw Filipinos in bright-colored shirts or pants walking on the pier. I felt like I was watching a foreign movie.

We got off the ship at 11 a.m. and arrived at the logistics quarters toward evening. On the way, I was impressed when I heard Filipino children sing Japanese war songs, such as Patriotic March well. I was surprised when they walked up to us and asked for cigarettes, saying, "We're friends!"

One day we went to work on airfield construction. It was the first time I had seen towns in Manila on my way to and from the airfield by truck. Tropical houses and clothes were unusual for me. Many Filipinos were chanting "Banzai" repeatedly raising their hands. Everything I saw and heard was a surprise to me.

The 139th Logistics Hospital was opened on December 12. I worked for Muñoz branch.

We left for Muñoz from Manila station by train. The small steam locomotive was like a 19th-century one. It started to run pulling four small carriages, blowing a whistle, "Bo-po-poh." Some Filipinos also boarded the roof of the train. They were having fun talking to each other, making funny cries. The train halted on the way.

"What happened?" "I'll see what the problem is," one of my fellow soldiers said and went to the locomotive.

　しばらくすると帰って来て、ニコニコ笑いながら、
「機関士が小便もしたいし、少し疲れたので小休止だって」

　なんだかんだと言いながら夕暮近くムニオスの駅と言うより１３９兵站病院分院になる建物の近くの野原に停ってくれた。皆それぞれ飛び下りて隊長・班長達に続いて歩く。
　門は両脇に通り路があり、門柱には水牛の頭が飾り付けられている。門前には農夫と水牛が水田を耕している銅像でもない土で造った像にペンキでも塗ったのか、その物ずばりと言う感じ。夕闇もせまり視界も定かでない所で牛の首。農夫の顔が造り物だけに無気味に感じた。門を入り一番近い２階建の家に入る。暗闇でローソクを灯したように想う。各班別に集まり夜食の握り飯を食べて寝る。

　翌朝、中隊長の訓示あり。私達の前に駐在していた部隊が造ったのか、2棟の兵舎があり、1棟には1から3班まで、別の棟には4、5、6班。私達は4班だった。班長は久世班長、杉兵長、松竹上等兵、三浦古兵、堀古兵、初年兵は堀口、長岡、藤岡、香月、小宮等。
　我々の分院の所在地は元ルソン島第一の農学校の跡で、道も広く両側にはマンゴーの樹の並木で教室が点々とあり、それぞれ独立したコンクリートで造られ立派な建物だった。室内は板張だった。

　毎日衛生材料の梱包をとき、所定の位置に運搬したり、藁蒲団を造ったり、患者収容の準備でいそがしく働いていた。

After a while, he returned smiling and said, "The engineer needed to use the lavatory and was a bit tired, so he took a rest."

As we talked about this and that, the train reached Muñoz toward evening. It stopped not at Muñoz station but in a field near the buildings that were to become the 139th branch hospital. We got off the train and followed team leaders or our company commander.

The gate had passages on both sides. The gatepost was decorated with a buffalo's head. In front, there was a statue, a man cultivating a rice field with a buffalo. It was not bronze but painted clay. They looked weird in the dim. I passed the gate and entered the nearest two-story house. We lit a candle in the dark. Each team gathered, ate rice balls for supper, and went to sleep.

The next morning, the company commander gave instructions. There were two barracks, seemingly made by the preceding company. Teams 1 to 3 stayed in one barrack and 4 to 6 in the other. I was in team 4. Our leader was Kuse. His men were Lance Corporal Sugi, Private First Class Matsutake, Veteran Miura, and Hori. Recruits were Horiguchi, Nagaoka, Fujioka, Katsuki, Komiya, and I.

Our branch hospital was on the site of the former 1st agricultural school in Luzon. The wide roads were lined with mango trees on either side. You could see classrooms here and there. Each was a separate, splendid concrete building. The rooms were boarded up.

Every day, we worked busily preparing to accept inpatients. We opened packages of hygienic materials and carried them to designated places. We made straw mats for the inpatients.

２週間位してからか初年兵の大半がデング熱に感染し、暑い比島で赤い顔して高熱を発しウンウンうなっていた。患者も収容しない内に自分達が病気になっては世話はない。デング熱も下火になり、軍規もきびしくなり、点呼の時は毎晩の様にビンタがとんで来た。

衛生兵としての教育も進み、戦友同士注射の稽古をしながら昭和19年の元旦を迎える。暑い所で熱い雑煮を汗だくになって祝うのも初めてだ。フンドシ一つになり胸から汗が流れ落ちるのでタオルを腹にまき、一枚は顔の汗をふいて、雑煮を食べるのも苦行だ。初年兵同士顔を見合わせ笑い合った。

間もなく患者も入院して来る様になり、病院らしい陣容を整えた。私は内科第３病棟勤務。３病棟の建物は凹型になり正面階段より左側が診察室、右の小部屋が事務室になった。軍医殿は江島士官と中島士官、班長は吉村康雄、金高三郎、山口量、橋口古兵、初年兵は浜辺、久原等だった。患者は総員130名くらいで担送1、護送2で、あとは独歩患者で主にマラリアの疑いで元気の良いのが多かった。

私は中島軍医殿の診断助手を命ぜられた。

患者の療養に当たる22歳の私は日々楽しく軍務に励んでいた。

Two weeks later, most recruits had dengue fever. We flushed, suffering a high fever in a tropical island. It was embarrassing that medics became sick before accepting patients. Soon we recovered from the fever. The rigor of military discipline was recovered too. They slapped us in the face at a roll-call every evening.

We had been trained to be medics, practicing giving an injection. Then, we celebrated New Year's Day of 1944. It was the first time we had eaten hot Zoni, sweating in a hot place. It was ascetic to eat it. We wore only a fundoshi, using one towel to wipe the face and another around the waist to stop sweat running down. We fellow soldiers looked and smiled at each other.

Soon, patients began to enter, the hospital was prepared for treatment. I worked for the 3rd ward of internal medicine. The building was concave-shaped. The examination rooms were on the left side of the front stairs. A small office room was on the right. Army doctors were Nakashima and Ejima. Sergeant was Yoshimura. Veterans were Kanetaka, Yamaguchi, and Hasiguchi. Recruits were Hamabe, Kuhara, etc. There were about 130 patients, including one stretcher case and two escort cases. Many of them, suspected of having malaria, could walk by themselves. I was ordered to help Dr. Nakashima.

I, 22 years old, took care of the patients each day pleasantly.

３月初め頃、日赤の看護婦さんが我が病院に転属されて来ると発表があり、どんな人が来るのかなぁと、ワクワクしながら初年兵達は寄ると、さわると、その噂話をしたものだった。内科3病棟には後藤、富樫、南野と3人の看護婦さんが勤務する事になり私達も紹介された。身内・肉親に会った様なほのぼのとした気持が私の胸の中を通過した。

看護婦が来て初年兵の気持がゆるんだと言う事で夕点呼のビンタの数もふえた。

衛兵、不寝番、病室週番と兵站病院での勤務も板に付いて来た。5月頃の雨季には並木のマンゴーの実も熟し、なんとも言えぬ芳香を放ち、また内地では味わう事の出来ない珍味だった。良く食べた。ビンタにも馴れ、勤務にも馴れ、患者の信頼も出来、楽しい勤務だった。

昭和19年の10月頃より衛生材料の分散を始めたトラックで警護兵として分乗し、よくあちらこちらと行動した。バンバンの小学校に行ったこともあり、その時は後日その地にバレテ峠を越えて自分達が転進してくるとは想っても見なかった。

In early March, it was announced nurses from the Japanese Red Cross Society would be transferred to our hospital. We, recruits, talked about them every time we saw each other, excitedly wondering what kind of people they would be. Three nurses, Goto, Togashi, and Nanno, came to take up their new posts in the 3rd medical ward. When I introduced myself to them, I felt something warm inside me, as if I had met my family or relatives.

Senior soldiers thought the recruits got loose on the nurses' arrival. So, they slapped us more often at a roll-call in the evening.

I was getting used to working as the guard, the night watch, and the weekly duty in the sickrooms. The mangoes in the avenue became ripe in the rainy season in May, giving off an indescribable aroma. They tasted delicious. They were what we couldn't appreciate in mainland Japan. We ate many mangoes. I got used to getting slapped and my work. Patients trusted me more. It was nice work for me.

In October 1944, the Japanese Army began to disperse sanitary supplies. I went to many places by truck to deliver them as a guard soldier. When I went to a primary school in Bambang, I never knew we would withdraw there later, crossing Balete Pass.

昭和16年9月 数え年20歳の著者
Masao Hamabe 19 years old
Sept. 1940

ムニオス病院勤務当時の筆者
at Muñoz in 1944

ムニオス分院内科病棟

ムニオス分院内科病棟　前列向かって左から3人目が筆者

At Muñoz in 1944. Front row, the 3rd from left is Masao Hamabe

昭和19年の暮近く、平和なムニオスの病院も戦車隊が入り戦車が木蔭に屯する様になり、あわただしい空気がみなぎる。

20年の元旦は雑煮を祝う事が出来た。

しかし、昭和19年の暮、20年の初頭より戦況も慌しくなり、私達の内務班も移動し、農学校の農作物の集積倉庫の大きい建物に入っていた。私達末端の初年兵には、何故そこに移動したのか他の事。近隣の様子など何も分らず目の前の事しか分らないので不安だった。

1月8日夜中、寝に就いた頃、週番下士官が「使役集合」

何だと聞いてみたら、

「マニラ陸軍病院よりの護送中の患者を乗せた汽車がギンバにおいてゲリラに襲撃され、孤立しているので只今より救助に向かう、武装して直ちに集合」

内務班にいても近況は分らず、もやもやの気分を発散させるのには持ってこいだとばかり、急いで支度をし、鉄兜、銃を持って教育隊前に集合し、弾丸を60発もらってトラックに乗車。

患者の中より1人陸軍士官学校出のバリバリの少尉殿が、単身患者の身でゲリラの集まる部落を突破して、病院に連絡に来て初めて分かったとのこと。その少尉殿が道案内のため、再度乗車して来た。運転台の屋根を軽機関銃の銃座にして2人の兵が射手として構えている。

(おれが機関銃を射ちたいのに……)

出発！

Toward the end of 1944, a tank corps came in, and tanks started to stay under the trees. So it was no longer peaceful in the Muñoz hospital. A tense atmosphere spread.

We could celebrate the feast on New Year's Day in 1945. However, from the end of 1944 to 1945, the war became severe. Our internal affairs corps moved to a large warehouse in an agricultural school. As recruits of low rank, we did not know why they moved. We were concerned because we didn't know anything about the situation.

It was midnight on January 8 when we got into bed. A noncommissioned officer of the week said, "Everybody, fall in!"

We asked him what had happened.

"Guerrillas attacked a train carrying patients from Manila Army Hospital. It was isolated in Guimba. We'll rescue them. Let's all assemble here, armed."

It was difficult to grasp the current situation in the internal affairs corps. I thought this would relieve my stress, and I got ready in a hurry. We gathered with helmets and guns in front of the Training Center, received 60 bullets each, then got on a truck.

One patient on the train, a brave second lieutenant, came to our hospital to inform us about the crisis. He graduated from the Military Academy. He broke through a village of guerrillas by himself. To show us the way he got on our truck. Two shooters armed the truck with a machine gun on the roof.

— I wished I had been a marksman. —

Let's go!

空を見れば星が無数に輝き日中の暑さも忘れ、ほほを打つ風も心地良かった。

案内の少尉殿が突然、

「みなさん、鉄カブトをかぶって顎紐をしめて弾込めして下さい。電線が切られている、状況は非常に悪い」

どんどん遠ざかりゆく途の電柱を見たら、電線は切れて地上にたれ下っていた。なるほど、士官学校出は違うなーと感心した。私も患者を看護する時、これからは周囲の状況には常に綿密な注意と鋭い観察力がいるなあ、それによって生死が分かれると思った。

どんどん進む内、前方に火の手が見え、その火の中に数人の人影がちらちらしていた。橋を焼いているらしい。

「停止、全員下車。車は向きをかえ帰る用意を」

と言う少尉殿の判断。

浜川上等兵が、

「浜辺ついてこい、橋まで行って見る」

私も2、3歩、歩きだしたら、少尉殿が、

「一刻も早く帰らないと危険だ、すぐ乗車」と大声を出した。

出発、トラックが動き出したら、すぐ左右からゲリラの襲撃を受ける。私達も応射する。彼我の銃声で敵の人数が分らなく多く感じた。顔を上げて見たら、くらやみの中に敵の銃口より発する赤い火がパッパッと見えた。運転中の松竹上等兵殿が尻を負傷し、一瞬車がグラっとして冷や汗をかく。

The sky was filled with countless stars twinkling after the day's heat had gone. A gentle breeze was blowing on our faces.

The second lieutenant suddenly said, "Everybody! Put on your helmet, fasten the chin strap and load your gun. I noticed the electric wires cut. The situation is terrible."

I saw the electric wires along the road cut and hung. He was what one would expect of a Military Academy graduate. I couldn't help admiring him. While caring for patients, I needed close attention and sharp observation. Life or death depended on it.

Going along, I could see a fire ahead and several figures through the fire. Apparently, they were burning a bridge.

"Stop and get out of the truck! Get the truck ready to turn back, men," the second lieutenant ordered.

However, PFC Hamakawa said, "Come with me, Hamabe. I'll visit the bridge to see how things are."

As I took a few steps forward, the second lieutenant shouted, "We're in imminent danger, there is no choice but to return! Get on the truck now."

Leave! As soon as the truck started moving, guerrillas attacked us from both sides. We fired back. Many gunshots made me feel there were more enemies. Raising my head, I saw fire flashing from the enemies' gun muzzles in the dark. The truck driver, PFC Matsutake, was shot in his buttocks, so the truck swung for a second. I broke out in a sweat.

次の日、徒歩にて再びおもむく。機関車が転ぷくしていたが人影なし。

引返す道中、アメリカ軍リンガエン湾上陸の報を聞き、いよいよ我々も戦いの火中に入ると身の引きしまる思いがする。

歴史的状況：

日本軍は、開戦劈頭マッカーサー大将の率いたアメリカ軍を追放し、フィリピンを支配していた。昭和19年秋、連合軍の進撃により、フィリピン近海のレイテ沖海戦で、日本海軍は壊滅的な打撃を受ける。連合軍は、ついにルソン島上陸作戦を開始した。日本陸軍は、山下奉文大将を派遣し、まずカガヤン河谷穀倉地帯で兵糧を確保しようとしたが、連合軍の進撃は予想以上に速かった。
そのため、北部山岳地帯に退避し、1日でも連合軍の本土上陸作戦を遅らせるべく、玉砕覚悟の持久戦を目指したのだった。

ルソン島の地勢：

ルソン島は、日本の本州島の半分弱の広さで、南側は関東平野ほどの平地になっている。
バレテ峠（標高900メートル）を越えた北東寄りには、北端に流れ込むカガヤン河に沿った穀倉地帯が続く。北西部は山岳地帯となっている。

We went back there on foot the next day. A locomotive had been overturned, and nobody was there. On our way back, We got information that the U.S. Army had landed in the Gulf of Lingayen. I felt tense when I realized I would plunge into the fire of war.

The historical situation in those days

The Japanese army expelled the U.S. forces led by General MacArthur at the beginning of the war and ruled the Philippines.

In autumn 1944, the Allied Forces devastated the Japanese Navy in the Battle of Leyte near the Philippines. Allied Forces began the Luzon landing operations. General Yamashita first tried to secure military resources in the Cagayan River granary. However, the Allied Forces advanced more quickly than they expected. The Japanese Army was forced to retreat to the northern mountain areas. So it aimed to delay the Allied Forces' landing operations in Japan, even one day, preparing for death.

Geographical features of Luzon

Luzon Island is almost half the size of Honshu Island in Japan. The southern part is flat, as large as the Kanto Plain.
(Cf. State of California: 423,970km^2 Luzon Island: 104,700 km^2)

From over Balete Pass (900 m above sea level), the northeast is a granary along the Cagayan River, flowing to its northern end.

The northwestern region is mountainous.

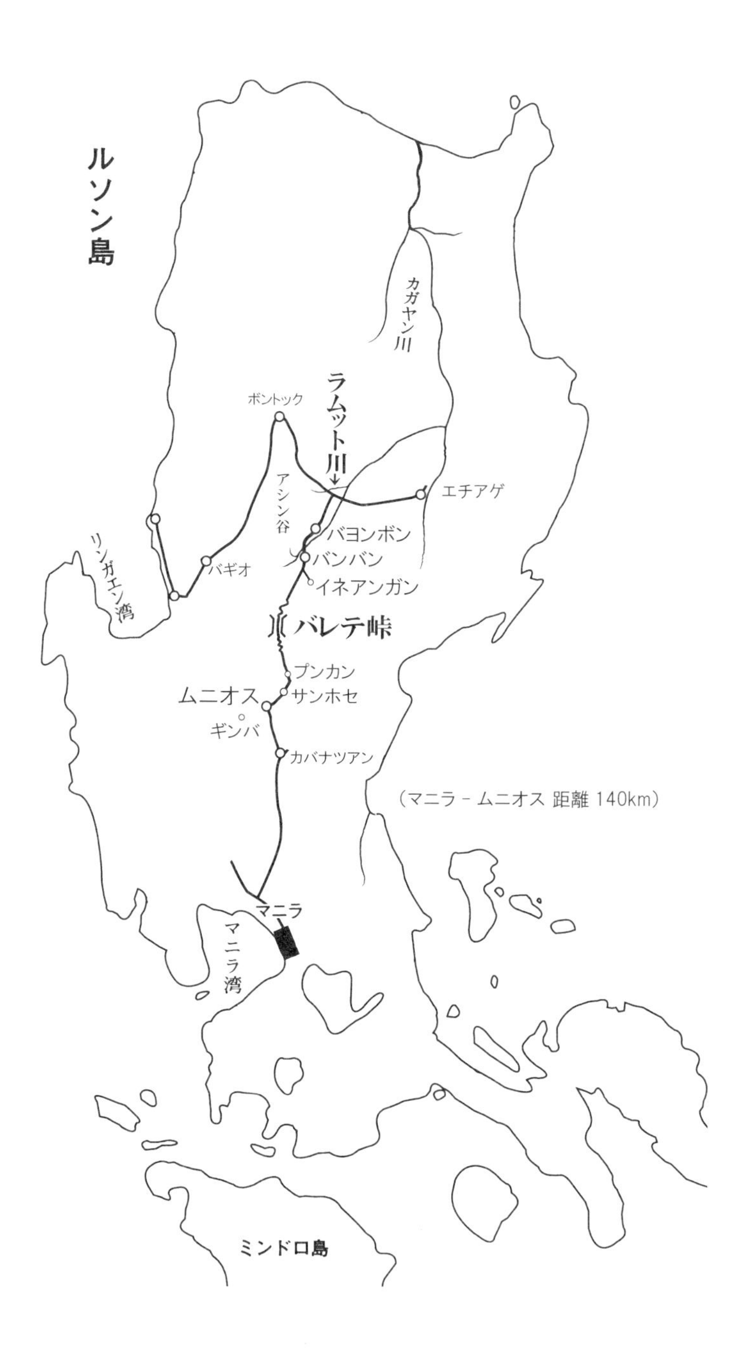
ルソン島
カガヤン川
ラムット川
ボントック
アシン谷
エチアゲ
バヨンボン
バンバン
リンガエン湾
バギオ
イネアンガン
バレテ峠
プンカン
ムニオス
サンホセ
ギンバ
カバナツアン
（マニラ - ムニオス 距離 140km）
マニラ
マニラ湾
ミンドロ島

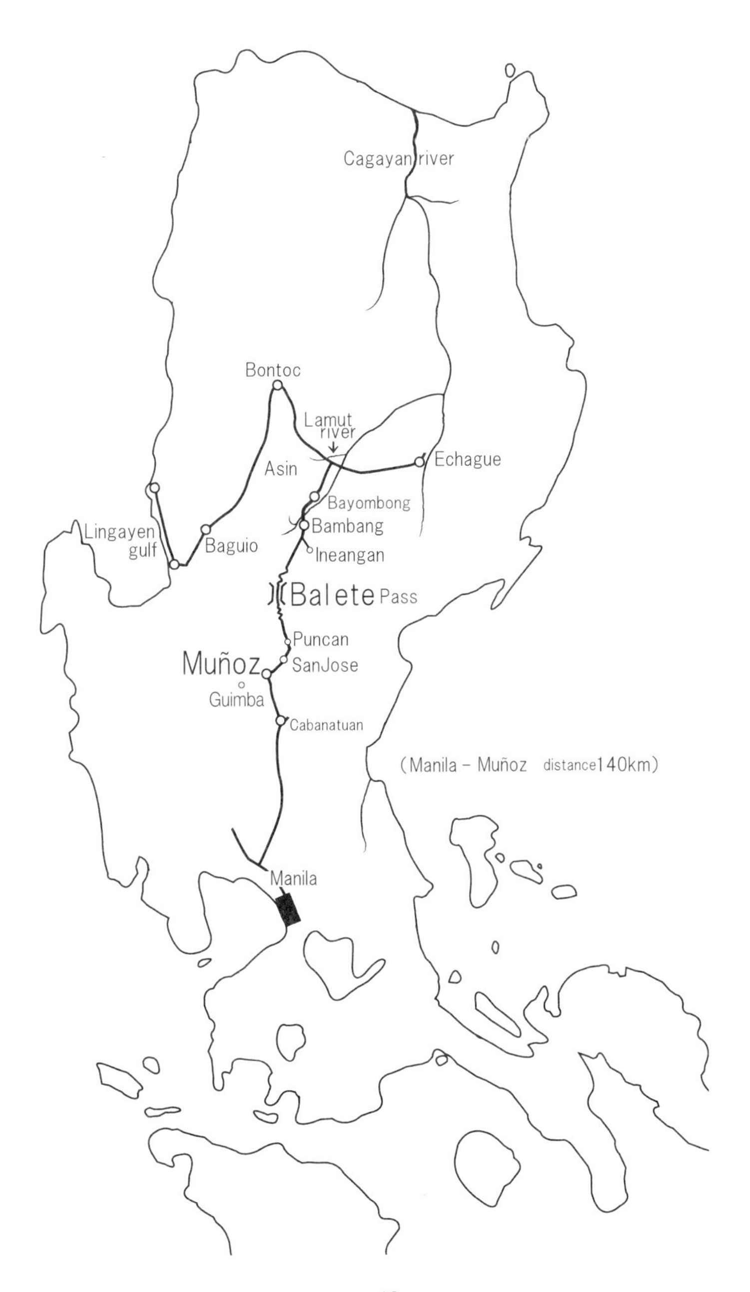
Cagayan river
Bontoc
Lamut river
Echague
Asin
Bayombong
Bambang
Lingayen gulf
Baguio
Ineangan
Balete Pass
Puncan
Muñoz
SanJose
Guimba
Cabanatuan
(Manila - Muñoz distance140km)
Manila

3　分水嶺　バレテ峠へ

部隊もいよいよ移動、酒保品のビール、甘味品、煙草は大盤振る舞い。一年余り過したムニオスをあとに、サンホセをすぎ山道を夜間プンカンに向かう。次々と戦友が出発、私も最後近く車に乗せてもらう。

翌未明プンカン着、小山の中腹の木蔭で寝る。

「浜辺、浜辺……」

と、ゆり起こされた。同年兵の久保吉蔵君が目の前に立っていた。

「なんだ」起きて見たら陽は高く10時頃だった。照り付ける太陽に汗をビッショリかいていた。

「飯だ」と、握り飯3個と漬物タクアン数切れ出した。昨夜より何も食べていないので急に空腹を感じ、ニャッと笑いながらほおばる。

「まだ炊事にはあるぞ」

「いやもう腹一杯だ」

「遠慮するな」

午後また久保君が握り飯を持って来た。今度はバナナの葉に丁寧にくるんでいた。

「今先発隊として30名募集している。行こうや」

「ええ、ここに残るより先に行った方が良かよ」

と2人は装具をかかえ集合場所に出た。

3 The Watershed, Balete Pass

Finally our troops started to move. The PX generously distributed a lot of beer, sweets, and cigarettes to us. We left Muñoz, where we had stayed for over a year. After passing San Jose, we headed for Puncan along a mountain road at night. The comrades left one after another. I got in the car last.

We reached Puncan at dawn the following day. I slept in the shade of a tree on a hillside.

"Hamabe, Hamabe!" Somebody shook me awake.

My fellow soldier, Mr. Kubo, was standing in front of me.

"What's up?"

It was around 10 a.m., and the sun shone high. I was drenched in sweat under blazing sunlight.

"It's brunch time." Kubo served me three rice balls and several pieces of Takuan (yellow pickled radish). I felt hungry suddenly because I had not eaten anything since the night before. I crammed them into my mouth with a smile.

"There's more food in the PX."

"No, thank you. I'm full," I said.

"Don't hesitate."

In the afternoon, Kubo brought me a few rice balls neatly wrapped in banana leaves. He said, "They are recruiting 30 participants as an advance party. Let's apply for it."

"Why not? It's better to go earlier than stay here."

Carrying army outfits, we went to the meeting place.

皆ニヤニヤしていたが緊張して一言の私語はない。やがて的野班長殿が来られ、

「整列」

皆バタバタと整列する。

「気を付けッ」

「休め」

「百姓の経験のある者、牛を使った事のある者は一歩前」

前に出ない者は私と久保君のみ。

「そのまま良く聞け、おれが指揮者で只今より、水牛車で出発する。水牛は向こうの草むらにおる元気の良いのを見つけてつれてこい。車はあそこだ、水牛を付け準備の出来た者より出発する」

私と久保君は顔を見合わせ、「班長殿、水牛を使った事はありません」（今さらどうにもならん、なんとかなるだろう）

「水牛をつれて来て準備をしろ」

おとなしそうなのをえらんで引張って来て車をつける。車には米、味噌、乾燥メノハが積まれ用意してあった。

皆は牛のすぐそばに手綱を取って立っていた。

「出発」的野班長の号令でゴトゴトと動き出す。私は手綱を長くして引張った。牛はおとなしくボッコボッコ歩き出した。私をなめるような気配はなく、ほっとして進む。

こうして、30人の兵が的野班長の指揮で目的地のアリタオ（バレテ峠の先）に向かう。

Everyone smiled but was tense and silent. Soon Sergeant Matono came and said,

"Fall in!"

Everyone lined up in a hurry.

"Attention!" "At ease!"

"Whoever was a farmer or used cattle, step forward".

Everyone except Kubo and I stepped forward.

"Guys, listen. I am the leader, and we'll now leave by water buffalo wagons. Bring vigorous ones from the grassy place over there. There're wagons there. Leave as soon as you've harnessed a water buffalo to your wagon and prepared."

We looked at each other. "Mr. Sergeant, we have never used a water buffalo," thinking inside, "We can manage it."

"Bring a water buffalo and get ready," said the sergeant.

Therefore, we selected a mild-looking one and harnessed it to our wagon. The wagon had been loaded with rice, miso, dried seaweed, etc. The other soldiers stood by the water buffalos, holding the reins.

"Let's go!"

Our wagons started to move, rattling under Sergeant Matono's command. I pulled the reins longer, and the buffalo started moving obediently. I was relieved because it was not defiant.

Thus 30 soldiers under Sergeant Matono headed for Aritao, which is beyond Balete Pass.

出発後何日目か、我々の横を一台の乗用車が通過。「アブナイ」と思う間もなく、街道荒しと言われるロッキードが飛来し機銃掃射の雨。草原にて隠れる場所なく水牛の腹の下にしゃがむ。

敵の爆撃日ましに激しく、日中の行軍は困難になる。バレテの峠を毎夜毎夜水牛を引きずる様にして登る。牛も人もだんだんと疲れ果てて来た。

小休止の時など道端に死んだ様に横たわる。水牛の動かぬ首に巻いたロープを肩にかけ引きずり引きずり登るので、牛の首筋は皮が破れ肉が出る様になり、1頭倒れ、また1頭と。途中酒保にいた淵上君がカルマタに乗り僕らを追い越していく。

「おーい頑張れよ！」と声をかけて。

1ヵ月あまりかかってバレテの頂上に至る。

Several days after our departure, a car passed by us. No sooner had I realized how dangerous it was than a Lockheed P38 appeared and strafed us. We called P38 the highway robbery. I crouched under the water buffalo because it was a grassy plain with no shelter.

The enemy air raids were getting more intense day by day, and daytime march became difficult. We marched up a slope to Balete Pass, dragging water buffalos every night. The soldiers and buffalos gradually exhausted themselves.

At the break, we lay by the roadside, half dead. As we pulled a rope wrapped around the buffalo's neck, its neck skin came off, and flesh appeared. The buffalos collapsed one after another. On the way, my fellow soldier Fuchigami, who was in charge of the PX, overtook us, saying, "Good luck!" He was riding on a Karumata, a small two-wheeled carriage with a pony.

It took over a month to reach the summit of Balete Pass.

後日談（昭和 60 年頃）

一三九会長崎大会の折、的野さんにお会いしました。「水牛を引張ってバレテ峠を越えアリタオの本隊に無事着くまでの事を誰かが寄稿してくれるだろうと思っていたら、君が書いてくれて有難う、自分の事を誰かが記憶していてくれた事は大変うれしい」とおっしゃっていました。昨年鬼籍に入られた由、茂木の三浦古兵殿よりうけたまわり心より御くやみ申し上げます。その当時も髭を生やされ、長身で百戦錬磨の士の風格あり、アルマゲルに着くまで色々の難関もありましたが、私達初年兵に一片の不安をいだかせる事なくすごしました。只々感謝。

A sequel in 1985.

I met Mr. Matono at the 139th Corps reunion held in Nagasaki city.

He said, "I was hoping someone would contribute to how we crossed Balete Pass and arrived at the main camp in Aritao. Thank you for writing about it! I'm pleased someone remembered me."

But, I heard about his death last year from Miura, former Private Veteran who lived in Mogi town.

I want to express my deepest condolences on the passing of the great sergeant. He was a tall man with a mustache and a veteran of battle-hardened samurai dignity. We recruits had various hardships until we reached Almaguer. But, he led us without making us feel uneasy.

I can't thank him enough.

4　アリタオ、バンバン

バレテ峠で一夜休んで朝早く一気に峠を下る。部隊に遅れた兵が三々五々と通る。ここからアリタオまでは平たん地である。休んでいると2、3人の兵が負傷してもどって来る。話を聞くと前方の道のまがった所で山の上からゲリラに狙撃されたとのことで、まず草むらに水牛をかくし一夜を明かすことにする。

車を草でおおい、草の下に寝る。班長の訓示、「夜中ゲリラの襲撃があるやもしれぬ、皆用心する様に」とのことであったが、幸い何事もなく夜が明け、また水牛車を引きずり歩く。

数日後アリタオに夜間到着。私はバンバン勤務との事で迎えに来ていた戦友とバンバンに行く。バンバンの街の小学校に病院を開設していた山田曹長殿に申告し下村班長の指揮下に入り、次の日より診断助手を務める。

ある日、四航軍の軍曹が大腿部を負傷して入院、病床日誌を作るため病室に行くと、

「おーい浜辺君ではないか」

と大声でわめき抱きついて来た兵がいた。内地の我が家の隣にいた柳川君である。負傷した軍曹の介抱に来ていたのだった。不思議な所で会うものだ。これから「エチアゲ」に向かうそうだ。元気な人であったが復員してみたら帰らざる人となっていた。

4 Aritao and Bambang

We took a night's rest at Balete Pass, then went down the pass without resting early in the morning. Some soldiers in groups of twos and threes, coming late, passed. The road to Aritao was flat. While taking a rest, I saw a few wounded soldiers returning. They said guerrillas had sniped them from the hill at a curve in the road ahead. So we hid the buffalos in a thicket and spent the night.

We covered the wagons with grass, and slept under them. The sergeant instructed us, "There may be a guerrilla attack at night, so be on your guard!" Nothing happened until dawn. We walked, dragging buffalo wagons.

Several days later, we reached Aritao at night. I was ordered to work in Bambang, so I went there with my comrade, who had come to pick me up. I reported my arrival to 1st Sergeant Yamada. He had opened a hospital at a former elementary school in Bambang. The next day, I started to be a medical examination assistant under Sergeant Shimomura's command.

One day, a sergeant of the 4th Aviation Corps, who had a wound on his thigh, was admitted. When I walked into the sickroom to make a clinical record, a soldier hugged me, shouting, "You must be Mr. Hamabe."

He was Mr.Yanagawa, who lived next to my home in Japan and came to take care of the sergeant. It was a coincidence to meet him in such a strange place! He was going to Echague. He was a cheerful person. However, after returning to my homeland, I found he had passed away.

◎バンバン勤務の想い出

勤務中１度牛車を引いてバトー橋を渡りバヨンボンに籾受領に行った時、バヨンボン着は、日没後で暗くなっていた。先程から声は聞こえるのに戦友の顔も姿も目に入らない。何かの光がやっと目に入る程度だ。

しまった、ビタミンＡの不足で「とり目」になった、心の中は不安と恐れがうずまき始めた。水牛の手綱だけはしっかり手に握りしめていた。どこで何して、どこを通って来たのか夜明にバンバンの街中に入っていた。

夜明けと同時に目も見えるようになった。やはり「とり目」だ。引率者の班長、同行の上等兵、古兵、同年兵皆いやな顔をして私をにらみつけていた。だいぶ失態をした様だった。

◎バンバン空襲

その後、山のふもとに小さな小屋を作り移り住み、山腹に毎日毎日防空壕を掘る。その頃は患者も4、5名となり戦友も本隊に帰ったのか20人位になっていた。毎日毎日空襲が激しくなり、防空壕から出る事が少なくなって来た。

バンバンには兵站司令部がある、司令官は中将だとか。

The memory of Bambang

We went to Bayombong across the Batu Bridge, towing the buffalo wagon to receive rice in the husk. When we arrived at Bayombong the sun had set, and it was already dark. Since a while ago, I could hear the voices of fellow soldiers but saw neither their faces nor figures. I could barely see some light.

Oh my God! I got night blindness because of vitamin A deficiency. Fear and apprehension swirled inside of me. I was gripping the reins of the buffalo. I didn't know where I was, what I did, or where I passed. We returned to Bambang at dawn.

My eyesight had recovered after daybreak. Just as I thought and I had gotten night blindness. The sergeant, a PFC, a veteran, and fellow soldiers all glared at me. I seemed to have committed a blunder.

Bambang Air Raids

After that, we moved to the foot of a mountain, making a small hut. We dug air-raid shelters in the mountainside every day. By that time, there were four or five patients. Some soldiers had returned to the main force, leaving about 20 soldiers. The air raids became intense day by day, and we spent most of our time in the air-raid shelter.

The logistics headquarters was in Bambang. I heard the commander was a lieutenant general.

ある日のこと、山の中腹の防空壕を出て、衛兵として山の入口で立哨していた。○○上等兵と２人、立哨と言うより監視と言うべきか、１日勤務の様だった。山の登り口に「タコツボ」を掘って空襲の時はその中に入る様にしていた。

午前中は何事もなく昼食後交代の時、街の中を流れている小川で水浴をする。

突然Ｂ25の編隊数10機がバンバンの空にあらわれる。橋の下にかくれる。やれやれ通過したと思う間もなく反転し、編隊をくずしたと見るや銃撃の雨を降らす。直線となりバンバンの街を灰にするが如く、数時間に亘り反復爆撃。

河の中を「這う」様にしてもどりタコツボに入る。私と上等兵殿は二つ掘ったタコツボに入っていた。爆撃は益々激しく遠く近く炸裂する音がひびく、付近にも数発炸裂し立木が倒れバリバリ燃え出し、あたり一面火の海と化す。

狭いタコツボの中に身うごきもならず、上に顔も出せず、うずくまって、いよいよ今生の別れと覚悟をきめた。駄目だと思いながらも、かなわぬ時の神頼み、村の鎮守の神様や八幡様が脳裡に浮かび、心の中で無事を祈っていた。また父母や弟妹達の事など想い出し、二度と会う事はないのかと思ったりしていた。

突然「浜辺、浜辺大丈夫か」と上等兵が声を掛けて来た。「ハイ、大丈夫です」と大声を出したら我に返ったようで恐怖感もうすらいで来た。

One day I was on sentry duty at the mountain entrance outside of the shelter at the mountainside. I worked with a Private First Class. It was all-day work, surveillance rather than sentry duty. We dug foxholes and would hide when bombed.

Nothing happened that morning. During shift change after lunch, I bathed in a brook flowing through the town.

Suddenly, dozens of B25 formations appeared in the sky of Bambang. I hid under the bridge. No sooner had I felt relieved at their disappearance than they turned back. As soon as they got out of formation, they showered a rain of bullets. Forming a straight line, they bombed repeatedly for hours as if they were trying to burn Bambang to ashes.

I came back into the foxhole, crawling through the brook. We were in individual foxholes. The bombing became more intense. Near and far, explosions rang out. Several bombs exploded near our foxholes, and the trees fell and caught fire. It turned into a sea of flame.

I crouched in a narrow foxhole, unable to wriggle or look to see how things were. I was prepared to die. One will pray to the gods in extremity. Although I thought it was useless, I prayed to my village shrine or the Hachiman shrine for safety. Remembering my parents, brothers, and sisters, I thought I would never see them again.

Suddenly, the PFC(Private First Class) asked me, "Hamabe! Are you OK? Hamabe!"

"Yes, sir! I'm all right," I answered in a loud voice. Shouting made me come to myself, and I felt my fear disappear.

炸裂音は間断なく、木の燃える音も激しい。上等兵の「浜辺大丈夫か」と呼ぶ声も段々と回数が増え泣き声になって来たようだ。今頃恐怖感におちいったのかと、なんとなくおかしくなった。3回に1回は聞こえないふりしてだまっていた。

2時間あまり街も山も灰になるほどの爆弾をおとす。爆撃の過ぎさった後は、バンバンの街は一軒の家もなくふき飛んでいた。黒煙があちこちに上っていた。

足元に小さなプロペラが落ちていた。なんだろうと思って戦友に聞いてみたら、爆弾についている物だそうだ。真っすぐ落下する様に。本当かな。

数日後、全員本隊に引上げる。

本隊に帰りムニオス時代の班長であった吉村軍曹の死を聞く。そして、ドイツの降伏、ルーズベルトの死の情報を聞く。

神国日本はまだまだ負けぬぞと思う。

毎日毎日患者が死んで行く。タンカで死体を運び穴に埋める。次々と死体がふえるので穴掘り作業が間に合わない様な状況下であった。

The sounds of explosions continued. The blazing sounds of trees were intense. I heard the PFC calling, "Hamabe, are you OK?" more often and becoming like a cry. I felt funny somehow when I realized he was getting frightened now. I didn't reply once every three calls, pretending not to hear.

The bombing continued for two hours until it burned the town and hills to ashes. After the air raids, all the Bambang houses had vanished. Black smoke was going up here and there.

A small propeller had fallen at my feet. I asked my comrade what it was. He answered it was a device attached to a bomb to fall straight. I wondered if it was true.

A few days later, all the members joined the main force. I heard of the death of Sergeant Yoshimura, who was our leader in Muñoz. We got information about Germany's surrender and Roosevelt's death. I thought Sacred Japan would not be defeated yet.

Some patients died daily. We carried the corpses on a stretcher and buried them in dug holes. The situation was that more and more people passed away, so we could not dig enough graves.

５　イネアンガン

イネアンガンの夜間動哨の事。

昭和20年5月中旬頃、バンバン地区は皆撤退してイネアンガンに帰隊した。夜間動哨勤務についていた時、砂糖きび畠の中で人の話し声と砂糖きびの茎のザワザワとゆれ動くのを目にして、ハッと立止って這って様子を見、「誰か」と声もかけて見たら、きびの茎のザワメキも止み、人がじっと息を殺しているような感じがした。

ゲリラか？　私が動哨している場所は病院の外であり、患者なら脱走になる。敵前逃亡は銃殺刑と習ったように記憶していた。ゲリラにしろ患者にしろ、姿を現わす様にしなければと思い、銃をすぐ撃てるようにして、大声で

「誰か、出てこい。出ないと撃つぞ！」

と叫んだら、銃のガチャガチャ鳴る音と私の声で、2人の男がきびの茎の間からのそのそ出て来て、土下座して、

「助けてください」「見逃して下さい」

小さな声を出して2人共、一生懸命頭を下げている。

我が病院の患者だった。私はゲリラと思って緊張していたので、一瞬ホッとして膝がだるくなった。

さてどうしたものか、一応脱走になる。それは当人達も充分、分かっているので助けてくれと頭を下げているのだ。

私も衛兵所に連行する気はなかった。

5 Ineangan

Sentry duty at night in Ineangan

Around mid-May 1945, all of us retreated from the Bambang area to Ineangan. When I was on sentry duty at night, I heard someone talking and saw the stalks of sugarcanes moving and rustling. I stopped and crept to see what was going on. I asked, “Who is it?”

The rustling disappeared. I felt someone holding their breath.

Guerrillas?

I was watching outside the hospital. If they were the patients, they were deserting. I remembered learning that desertion in the face of the enemy resulted in death by shooting. I thought I had to make sure they were there, whether guerrillas or patients. Getting ready to shoot at any moment, I shouted, “Who is it? Come out, or I’ll fire a gun!”

At the gun clattering and my voice, two men came slinking out between the stalks. They fell on their knees to call for help.

“Please help us. Please overlook us.” They begged me in a tiny voice and were desperately bowing down.

They turned out to be our patients. I had been on my guard against guerrillas, so I felt my knees giving way with relief.

Well, how should I deal with them? They are deserters anyway. They understood it. That’s why they’re begging me for help.

I could not bring myself to take them back to the guardhouse.

イネアンガンの病院は竹ヤブの中の竹で編んだ家に患者を収容していた。

衛兵所の前には「どぶ川」があり、小さな木の橋がかかっていた。病院と言っても名ばかりで患者がおり、軍医殿や衛生兵、看護婦がいて患者の治療に当っている。ヤブの中と形容する方が似合っている。食糧も充分とは言いがたく、砂糖黍畠が近くにあれば脱走しても食べたいと思うだろう。このまま別れてもまた誰かに見つかったら大変だ。

「だまっておれについてこい」と言って衛兵所の近くまで来て様子を見る。

戦友達は疲れ果てたように思い思いの方を向いて座っていた。星あかりはあったが無事通過。

「二度と出ては駄目だぞ」と言うと、2人は本当によろこんで、何回も何回も頭を下げて、

「衛生兵殿、お名前をおしえて下さい。お願いします」と言うのを振切って別れた。

その後、私も2人の顔は暗くて良く見えなくておぼえていない。2人も私の顔はおぼえていないと思うと、すぎさってから急に私の頭の中に心配が一気に吹き出して来た。かりにも脱走してきび畠に潜み食べていた者を見のがして病院内まで連れて来て上官に報告しないということは、どういうことになるのか。何日かは不安な日々だった。

At the hospital in Ineangan, the patients were in a bamboo-knitted house in a bamboo thicket. In front of the guardhouse, there was a "muddy ditch" with a small wooden bridge. It was a hospital in name only. The patients were taken care of by army doctors, nurses, and medics. It might be better to call it "a place in a thicket".

It was hard to say the food was enough. As there was a sugarcane field nearby, they might feel like escaping from the hospital to eat. I could have set them free, but it was clear they would be in big trouble if someone found them.

I said, "Follow me in silence." and went near the guardhouse to see what it was like there. My war comrades sat in their way, exhausted. It was a starry night, but we passed safely.

I told them, "You must not escape again!"

They rejoiced and bowed to me many times, saying, "Mr. Medic, please tell me your name."

But I broke away from them without telling my name.

I did not remember their faces because it was dark. I thought neither of them remembered my face. However, as time passed, I suddenly began to worry. What would become of me? I overlooked the men who had escaped to eat sugarcane. Then I took them to the hospital but didn't report the incident to my superiors. I was uneasy for several days.

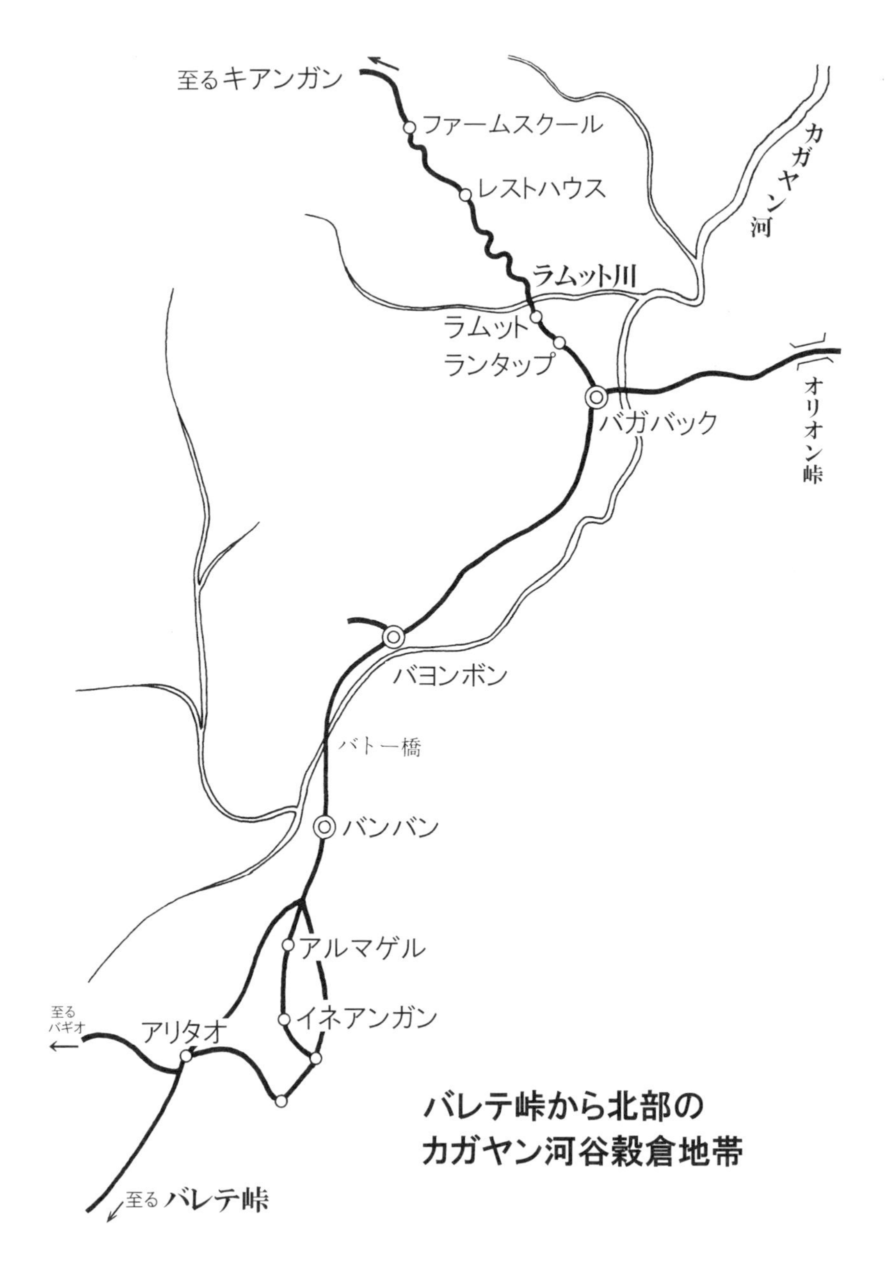

バレテ峠から北部の
カガヤン河谷穀倉地帯

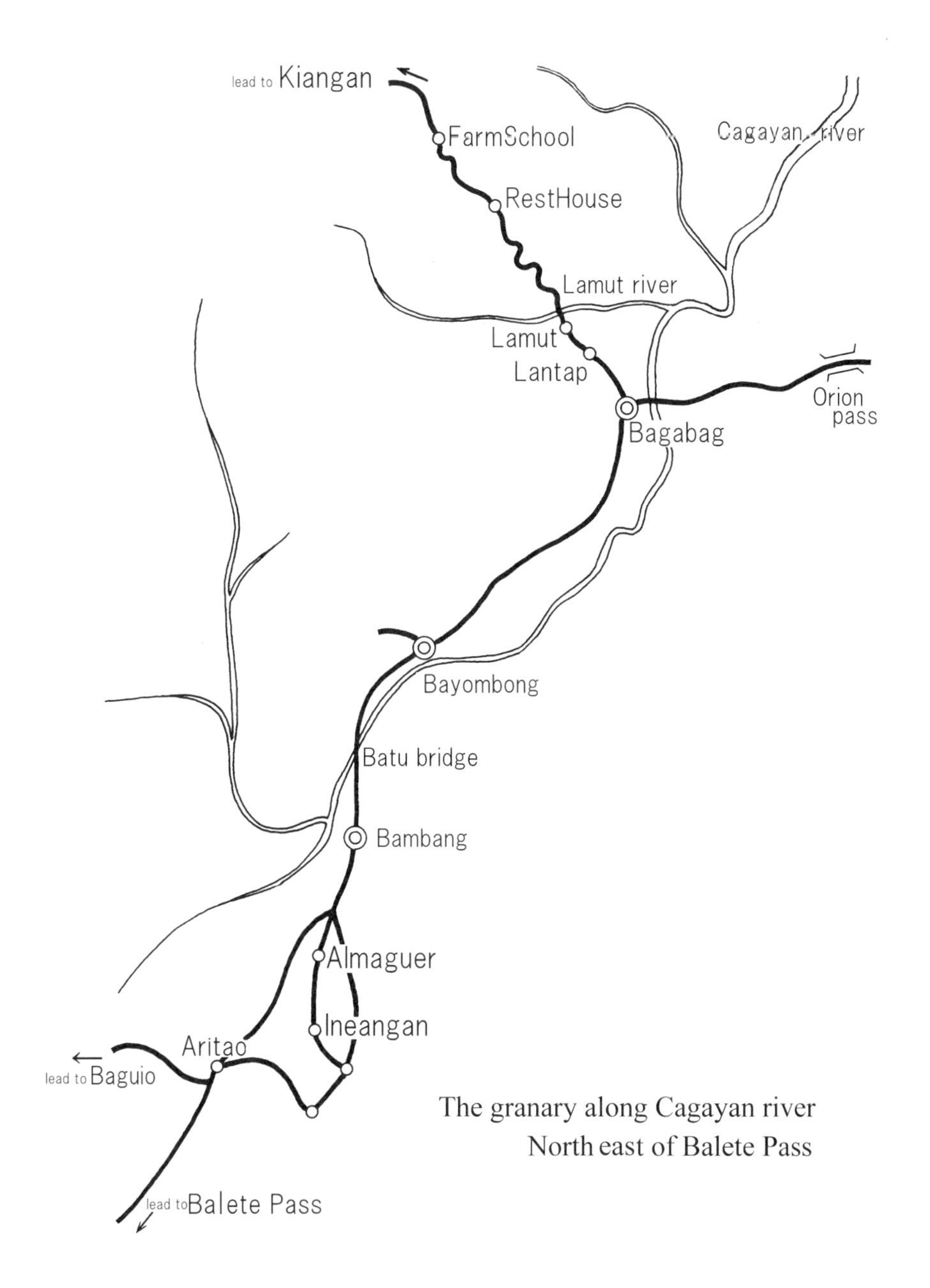

The granary along Cagayan river
North east of Balete Pass

６　「死の谷」アシンに向かう

６月１日、半年余り戦い続けたバレテの戦線ついに崩れる。

６月２日夜より急きょ重傷患者を竹ヤブの中の病室よりトラックの入る道まで出す。50メートル歩いては坐り込むのをドナリドナリ歩かせる。担架で運びトラックに乗れないでもがいているのをかかえ上げ放り込む。一人でも多く乗せようと私たちは必死だ。

６月３日夜、水田軍医殿を長として独歩患者50名を引率、班長（下士官）１名、兵３名で、次の目的地レストハウスに向けイネアンガンを出発。

死の谷への第一歩を踏み出す。

独歩患者とは言え、皆よわり果てた病人などで歩みは遅々として進まず、敵戦車の音が聞こえる様で気がせく。休もうとする患者等を時には怒り、時にはやさしく、一歩でも二歩でも進ませようと必死で歩む。

私等の歩いている道は国道五号線。Ｂ25の監視がきびしく夜間の行動しか取れないので、昼間は道端の木かげに休み、夜歩きつづける。南下する戦闘部隊と北上する我々バレテをおわれた部隊、兵隊街道は部隊でごった返しで、ともすれば迷子になりかねない患者も出る。

6 To Death Valley the Asin

On June 1, the front of Balete Pass, where the Japanese Army had continued fighting for half a year, finally collapsed.

On the night of June 2, we rushed critically ill patients from the bamboo grove's sickroom to a road where a truck could come. Some patients had trouble walking and rested every 50 meters. I had to shout to encourage them to walk. We carried some of them on stretchers, and needed to lift and throw them onto a truck. We made a desperate effort to take as many patients as possible.

On the night of June 3, we left Ineangan for our next destination, Rest House. Army surgeon Mizuta led a sergeant, three soldiers, and 50 ambulatory patients.

It was our first step into the Valley of Death.

Even though they were ambulatory patients, everyone was exhausted. They walked so slowly that I was afraid I would hear the enemy's tanks. I had to rush them when they wanted to rest, sometimes angrily or tenderly. I desperately made them advance even one step or two further.

It was National Highway Route 5. We must take night action because of the B25's strict surveillance. We rested under trees on the roadside in the daytime and walked at night. The road was busy, with the combat troops going south and our logistics unit going north. Some patients became lost.

誰が考えたのか車のタイヤを細長く切り火をつけて燃やすと「タイマツ」代わりになる。何百何千と言う兵が一人一人タイマツを持って歩いているので、後を振返って見ると戦勝祝のタイマツ行列の様だ。「きれいだなあ」と誰かが言う。

昼は空襲が激しく寝る事が出来ない。最初はビクビクしてなかなか寝つく事が出来なかったが、神経が麻痺したのか次第にグウグウ寝る様になる。

Someone cut the tire of a car into long thin pieces and burned them. It was a good "torch" substitute. I had no idea who created it. Thousands of soldiers were walking with a torch in each hand. So, it looked like a torch parade for a victory celebration. One soldier said, "It's beautiful!"

We couldn't sleep because of furious air raids during the day. I was so nervous and could not fall asleep at first, but later, slept well. I was exhausted, so I became insensitive.

7　ラムット川の惨劇

７日夜からものすごい豪雨が昼も夜も続き闇夜を手さぐりで歩く様になる。下着まで濡れ装具の毛布も水にぬれ重く、肩にくい込む毛布を半分に切る。

８日の夜明け近くバガバックに入る。道は日本の部隊と在留邦人で混雑していた。前方の車が故障をおこしたのか、車の列がとまる。運よく１台の空トラックが私等の横にいた。運転者にかけより「オーイ、１３９兵站病院だ、患者を50人連れている、乗せて下さい」とたのむ。車は患者輸送隊であったので快く「早く乗せろ」と言われ急いで患者を乗せる。士官殿は助手席に乗る。我々も乗りたかったのだが50人も１台に乗ったので遠慮する。トラックは動き出した。ヤレヤレと重荷を降ろした様な気持になる。

6月９日

バガバックから６キロ北西にラムット川（ランタップ川）と言う川がある。ラムット川はひどく増水していた。

追いたてられた在留邦人部隊の群が、夜の街道にあふれ、橋を渡るために一点に集中したので人人人、車車車でごった返していた。

歩いて渡る者、橋は一杯、夜明けは近い。明るくなるとB25のえじきとなる。

夜は白々と明け始めた。急きょ、橋を離れ街道より遠のき山に入る。

7 The tragedy of the Lamut River

Since the night of the 7th, it had continued to rain heavily night and day. We groped our way in the dark night. I got soaked in my underwear. The blanket of the outfit got drenched too, and it got so heavy on my shoulders that I cut it in half.

We went into Bagabag toward dawn on June 8. The road was crowded with Japanese troops and residents. A line of cars got stuck. A car ahead might have broken down. Luckily, there was an empty truck beside us. I ran up to the driver and said, "Hey, we are members of the 139th Logistics Hospital. We have 50 patients. Please give us a ride."

He replied readily, "Let them get on in a hurry."

The truck was a patients' transport unit. I hurried the patients onto it. The officer sat beside the driver. Fellow soldiers and I wanted to get on, but we declined because 50 patients got on. The truck started moving. I felt relieved of my burden.

On June 9.

There was a river called Lamut or Lantap, 6 km northwest of Bagabag. The Lamut River had been rising.

The area was jammed with people and cars, because they flocked to the bridge to cross it. The bridge was full of people trying to cross it on foot. Dawn was near. They would fall victim to B25s when the day broke.

Dawn was breaking. We left the bridge to the hillside from the road in a hurry.

夜が明けて見ると、この附近は広々とした平原地帯で密集した林も窪地もない所だ。小さな木の蔭に天幕を張り、雨の中にじっとうずくまって一日を過す。

後日聞いた話であるが、比島敗走の悲劇といわれる修羅地獄がこの橋で起こったようである。我々は、橋を離れていたので難をのがれたが、川岸には多くの部隊、在留邦人が砲撃・爆撃の餌食になった。泣きさけぶ子供や老人、川に飛び込む兵。米軍は部隊の渡河点と見て河岸一帯を撃ちまくったのだった。

米機が帰り爆撃が止んだので街道の方に出る。鉄橋は爆撃でこわされ、河原にかけられた仮橋は押し流され、通行不能になっている。

朝から何も口に入れていない。米はない、腹はへる。

「班長殿、何か食う物を見つけて来ます」

と同年兵の〇〇君と出かけ、米を民家よりさがし飯を炊いてもどってみたら班長殿の姿が見ない。 我々が道を間違えたのか。

附近を探すうち､小さな竹ヤブの中に入る。入ってみてびっくり、竹ヤブの中は小さなマーケットをひっくり返した様な有様。将校行李あり、軍票の箱詰、米、味噌・干野菜・肉・マッチなど山と積まれている乗用車もある。橋を渡るため皆ここに残したものと思われる。マッチをゴム袋につめ、米2、3合、野菜、肉等を背のうに入れ橋の所に行くが橋は渡れない。

I noticed this area was a spacious plain without dense forests or hollows. We pitched a tent under a small tree and spent a rainy day crouching still.

I heard later the tragedy of evacuation in the Philippines had occurred on this bridge that day. We had left the bridge before dawn so we escaped danger. The bombardment and bombing killed many troops and Japanese residents at the riverside. The victims included children crying for help and old people. Some soldiers jumped into the river. The U.S. Forces had inferred the riverbank was a crossing point, so they fired there.

After US planes flew away and the bombing stopped, we went to the highway. They destroyed the iron bridge and washed away the temporary bridge. There was no way to cross the river.

I had not eaten any food since that morning. There was no rice left. I was hungry.

"I'll go look for something to eat, Mr. Sergeant!" I went out with one of my fellow soldiers. We found rice in a house and boiled it, but the sergeant was not there when we returned. Had we come back to the wrong place?

While looking for him, we walked into a small bamboo thicket. We were surprised at what we saw. It was like a messy small market. There were some military trunks and boxes with military currency. Some cars were piled high with rice, miso, dried vegetables, meat, matches, etc. Seemingly, some soldiers had left them there to cross the bridge. I put some matches in a rubber bag, rice of around 500g, vegetables and meat in my backpack. We went to the bridge, but we couldn't cross it.

　暗くなるにつれ、各部隊の兵が街道に集まる。橋の所に行ったりもどったり、渡れないと思っていてもじっとしておれない。敵は間近に来ている。

　我等2人も群の中にうろうろする。見習士官殿が長で我々部隊の兵が3、40名通るのに会う。合流するも同じ事のくり返し、その内6、7名はぐれてしまう。
　同年兵ばかり。
「浜辺、どうしよう」
「皆ムニオスの仲間だ、気が合う、ええ、どうにかなるさ」
と先程の所に案内して皆それぞれ食糧を背のうに入れ、空いた民家に入る。火をたき、皆裸になってぬれた服をほし、肉を食い酒を呑み飯を腹一杯食う。ムニオスを出発以来の御馳走である。盆と正月が一緒に来た様だと笑う。腹がふくれて目の皮がたるむと、いつしか皆グッスリと深い眠りに入る。

　迫撃砲の砲弾が隣の家に命中した音にビックリさせられ眠りをさます。次々と破裂する。真暗やみの中でローソクに火をつける。装具を身に付ける。
「灯を消せ！　馬鹿野郎！」
と怒鳴られ、火を消して街道に飛び出す。
　街道には○○部隊集合所、○○中隊集合所と書いたノボリがあちこちに立ち連絡兵が走り回っている。

As it was getting dark, the soldiers from each unit gathered on the highway. We went back and forth to the bridge. We knew it was impossible to cross it, but we could not stay still. The U.S. Army was approaching us!

Walking around the crowd, two of us met 40 members of our unit led by a probationary officer. We joined them and tried to cross the bridge but couldn't. Then, six of my fellow soldiers, including me, strayed from our unit.

"What should we do? Hamabe! "

"We're fellow soldiers in Muñoz. We're congenial friends! It'll come out all right."

I took them to "the supermarket in a bamboo thicket". We put food in our backpacks and went into an empty house. Taking off our wet clothes, we made a fire to dry them, ate meat, drank alcohol, and ate enough rice. It was the best meal since we left Muñoz. Everyone smiled, saying, "It's like the Bon Festival and the New Year."

A full stomach induced deep sleep before we noticed it.

We woke up in surprise to loud noise. Mortar shells hit a house next door and exploded one after another. We lit a candle in total darkness and put on our outfits.

"Put out the light! Idiot!"

Someone yelled at us from outside. We extinguished the candle and rushed out to the highway.

Flags mentioning a meeting place of a certain unit or company stood here and there on the highway. And messenger soldiers were running around.

橋の修理はとうとう出来ず、行くべき所を見うしなってしまった。我々は途方にくれるが時は2時、3時と刻々と過ぎる。

「こら、そこの兵隊何をしている」大きな声でどなられ、
「ハイ、衛生兵です」
「何をグズグズしている、敵は夜明にはこの線まで来るぞ。我々はここで死守する、早く消えろ」と、若い中尉殿が軍刀をわしづかみにして立ちはだかり、
「見ろ」
道の端々には、機関銃、対戦車砲などすえ、一矢むくいんものと、兵隊も緊張した面もちでしゃがんでいる。
雨もすっかり上がり白々とした月あかりの空を見る。よゆうもないが国道五号線はクッキリと目にうつる。川が氾濫して水が街の中に入って来ている。
我々もここで死のうと思うが、
「○○兵站の兵500名位、憲兵隊の案内で川上に登るため集合しているからそれに合流せよ」と先程の中尉殿の当番兵に知らされる。
武運長久を祈って別れ、兵站部隊の集団の中に入る。

川にそって道が川上にのびている。水があふれ、道は見えぬけど腰まで水につかって進む。右手の川より氾濫した水が流れて来るので、ともすれば足をとられそうになりながら2時間あまり歩いたら、水の中からぬけ出す。ぬれたまま皆ブッ倒れる様にして眠りこけた。

After all, the bridge could not be repaired, and we couldn't find a place to go. Time passed while we were at a loss what to do. It was already 3 o'clock.

"Hey, you! What are you doing?" we were yelled at.

"Yes, sir. We're medics."

"Hurry! The enemy will be coming to this line by dawn. We'll defend here to the last. Leave now!" A young first lieutenant stood, clutching his military sword, and said, "Look!"

By the side of the road, the soldiers were crouching with tense looks on their faces. They placed machine guns and antitank guns, etc., hoping to retaliate against the enemy.

It had stopped raining altogether, and I saw a bright moonlight in the sky. I remained tense, but I saw National Highway Route 5 clearly. The river had overflowed and flooded the town.

We thought we would die here.

But then, the lieutenant's messenger soldier came and said, "About 500 soldiers of a logistics corps are gathering to go upstream under military police guidance. Join them."

We wished him good luck in battle and parted, then joined the logistics corps.

The road extended upstream along the river. The road had flooded, but we advanced, waist-deep in water. As the water overflowed from the right side of the river, I nearly tripped in water. After a two-hour walk, we found ourselves on a dry road. All of us slept like a log in our wet clothes.

日が昇り、焼きつく様な南国の太陽が照りつける。部隊は川岸に集結し隊長の訓示を受けていた。幾分か川幅もせまくなっていたが土色に濁った水は、ゴウゴウと音を立ててものすごい勢いで流れている。部隊はこの川を渡る決心の様だ。

水泳に自信のある兵は泳ぎ渡ろうとしてたちまち急流に押し流され、その生死は不明である。

部隊一の水泳の名人が選抜され、ロープを体に巻き付け川に飛込む、皆かたずをのんで見守る。30メートルほど流されながらも向こう岸に泳ぎつき大木にロープを巻き付け、こちら側も巻き付けピーンと張ったロープにぶら下がりながら一人ずつ渡る。途中何人かはロープを握る力をなくして流れの中に消えて行った。

最後に隊長がロープの端を体に巻き付け川に飛込むと向こう岸の兵隊が一生懸命引く。

我々５名だけが取り残される。シューンシューンと音を残して敵迫撃砲弾が頭上を飛ぶ。泳いで渡るか、ここで自決するか、相談をする。

○○君は「自決するより泳いで渡ろう、流されて死んでも元々だ」

皆、その気になって仕度を始める。樺太育ちの私は泳げないので皆の仕度を見ている。

The sun had risen. The scorching sun in the southern country was beating down on us. At the riverbank, the leader instructed the soldiers. That part of the river was narrower, but roaring muddy water was streaming. They seemed determined to cross this river.

Some confident swimmers among the soldiers tried to swim across it. But the torrent washed them away instantly, and it was unknown whether they were alive or dead.

The best swimmer in the unit was selected. He wound a rope around his body and jumped into the river. Everyone watched him, holding their breath. Though the torrent carried him away for about 30 meters, he swam to the opposite bank. Then he tied the rope to a large tree. They tied the other end to a tree on our side. They crossed the river one by one, hanging from the taut rope. Some soldiers lost their power to grip it on the way and disappeared into the torrent.

Last, the leader wound the rope's end around his body and jumped into the river. The soldiers on the opposite side pulled the rope with all their might.

Only five of us were left behind. The enemy's mortar shells flew over our heads, leaving a whizzing sound. We talked about whether we would swim across the river or commit suicide here.

One of us said, "We'd rather swim across the river than kill ourselves. We'd be none the worse for trying and die."

They put their minds on crossing the river and began to prepare. I couldn't swim because I grew up in Karafuto, north of Hokkaido, so I was watching everyone getting ready.

「浜辺なぜ仕度をしない？」
「泳げないんだ。１人残るから皆渡ってくれ元気でな。これが皆との最後だ」
「それは駄目だ、浜辺１人残して行けるものか、死ぬ時は皆いっしょに死のう」
　皆手を握り合って今後の行動を考える。
　この時ほど苦楽を共にした戦友の心意気を感じたことはありませんでした。

"Hamabe! Why don't you get ready to swim?"

"I can't swim. So I'll stay here. Go ahead and cross the river, guys! Good luck. This is the last time I'll see you."

"No! We can't leave Hamabe alone. When dying, let's die together."

We considered what to do, holding each other's hands. Never had I felt the spirit of the comrades with whom I shared many hardships and joys as I did.

8　本隊を追って

私達は渡河点を求め、出発せんとしていた荒木兵団にまぎれ込み、上流に向かって出発する。その後兵団とも別れる。

ひとまず腹ごしらえをしよう。昨夜からの雨で燃えるような枯葉もなく、竹を楊子の様に小さくけずり煙の出ないように少しずつ燃やしながら飯をたく。腹がふくれてくると気も落ちつき、追いつめられた恐怖感も薄らぐ。

先程の部隊が落としていった油紙に印刷された地図があったので地図をたよりに今後の行動を語る。先ずリーダーを決めよう。

私が皆の賛同でリーダーとなる。地図によれば川は上流からバガバッグの街に流れ、道はバガバッグより左にまがりファームスクール、レストハウス、キャンガンに続いている。川を渡り、まっすぐ北に向かって行けば何日かかるか分からんが、道に出る。川を渡る事が先決問題となる。

渡河点を見つけるため、私等は川に沿って上流の方に歩き始める。小さな山道を2日ほど歩く。附近一帯は家もなく田畑もなく樹木のはえ繁ったさみしくなる様な静かな所だった。

2日目の午前10時頃か、前方にチラチラと人影が見える。皆を木蔭に待機させ、気づかれぬ様に注意しながら近づいて見ると日本人だ。

「おーい大丈夫だ」皆を呼ぶ。

8 In pursuit of the main force

We mingled with the Araki Brigade, about to leave, looking for a crossing point on the river, and left for upstream. Some time later, we parted from them.

Let's eat something anyway. There were no burnable dry leaves from last night's rain. So, I cut bamboo into small pieces like toothpicks. I burned them little by little to keep from smoke, and cooked rice. When we were full, we felt relieved, and our fear of being cornered eased.

We discussed relying on an oil paper map that the preceding unit had dropped. First, let's decide the leader.

They selected me the leader. According to the map, the river flows in Bagabag. The road turns left there and leads to Farm-school, Rest-house, and Kiangan. If we cross the river and head straight north, we will come to a road, though there is no telling how many days it will take. So, we should first cross the river.

We started walking upstream along the river to find a crossing point. We walked on a path for two days. It was a lonely and quiet place with no houses or farms, but trees grew thick all around.

On the second day, around 10 a.m., I caught a glimpse of some figures ahead. I got everyone to stand by under a tree, and I approached cautiously to avoid being noticed.

They turned out to be Japanese.

"Hey! No problem," I called my fellows.

マニラの軍司令部で働いていた若い女性が10人位と男性3人程で、リーダーは白い綺麗なあごひげの人品いやしからぬ50くらいの人だった。渡河点を物色中の様で女性群は木蔭にうずくまり、男性が鉈やのこぎり等で木を切り倒している。この辺は河幅もせまくなって一泳ぎで渡れそうな所で、両端の大木を切り倒し、中央で結んでまず女性が渡り、我々もと思っていたが急流に大木もアッと思う間もなく流される。幸い女性等が渡った後であった。

私もおそるおそる河に入ってみる。水位は首くらいでどうにか歩いて渡れそうだ。装具を頭に乗せ2、3回往復して対岸に渡ることが出来た。

ホッとして四方を見渡す。先程の人々は姿も見えず、水田が広々と続き、遠くに小さな森らしいものがチラホラ見える位でどこをどう行くのか、行ったら良いのか皆腰を落として思案にくれる。

何はともあれ田のあぜ道を北に向かって歩く。

1、2時間歩いたら虎兵団の電話線が田の中を通っているのが目につき、それをたよりに歩く。途中多くの人が通ったと思われる草をふみ倒した道らしいものを見付け、それに沿って歩く。

何時間くらい歩いたのか山々に夕暮れがせまりつつあり、人影もなく物音もなく静かなこの世の生物の息もたえてしまった様な雰囲気で薄気味が悪い。背筋に悪寒が走る。

There were three men and ten young women who had worked at the military headquarters in Manila. The leader was a 50-year-old gentleman with a neat white beard. Women were crouching in the shade while men were cutting down a tree using a hatchet and saws. The river's width was narrow here, and we felt like we could swim across. We cut down the big trees on both banks and tied them in the middle. The women crossed first. We wanted to follow them, but a rapid stream washed away the trees in a flash. Luckily it was after the women had finished crossing.

After a while, the current became milder. I tried to get into the river. The water was up to my neck, and I thought I could walk across. Putting outfits on our heads, we were able to cross the river back and forth a few times.

I was relieved and looked around. The people mentioned before were not visible. The rice fields were spacious and continuous. I could see what appeared to be groves dotting in the distance. Sitting down, we racked our brains about where and how we should go. Anyway, we walked along a ridge between rice fields toward the north.

After walking an hour or two, I saw a telephone wire of the division named TIGER set up over rice fields. We followed it. On the way, I found a grassy track that seemed to have been trodden by many people. We walked along it.

While we were walking for several hours, dusk fell over the mountains. There was neither a sound nor a figure. I felt creepy because it was an atmosphere as if all the world's creatures had died out. A chill ran down my spine.

日も落ち暗くなってやっと一軒のアバラ屋を見つける。暗がりに四つんばいになって中に入る。牛小屋の様な所で、皆一時、四つんばいになったまま息をとめ、中の様子をうかがう。目がなれるにしたがってボンヤリながら見える様になる。先ほどまで多くの兵士がいたと思われる。日の丸の旗にくるんだ米だとか、ハンゴウの中ブタ等が落ちていた。火を灯し夕食を用意し何日ぶりかで屋根の下で寝る。

カンカンと照りつける南国の太陽の光に目をさます。昨夜ぐっすり寝られたので幾分元気が出た。

小さな人間１人通れる様な山道が一本北東に向ってまがりくねって続いていた。人影はなくても太陽は光り輝き、鳥はさえずり遠くの方ではかげろうが立ちこめ、戦を忘れた田舎の、のどかなたたずまいである。が、本隊から離れた我々の心の中には早くとせき立てられるものがあり、歩を早くする。

それから数日、山を越え河を渡り谷を下り、毎日毎日北へ向かって歩いても歩いてもなかなか本街道に出ることが出来ない。

途中友軍が通ったのだろうか、2、3合くらいの米が落ちていたので食糧には不自由はなかったが、副食もなく米だけ食べて雨にぬれ、また乾きするので体力がだんだんおとろえてくる。

洋服がむれて足に「潰瘍」が出来る。

After sunset as it got dark we finally found a shabby house. In the dark we went inside crawling on all fours. It was like a cattle shed. Holding our breath on all fours, we waited to see how things were inside for a while. As our eyes adapted, we could see things dimly. There seemed to have been many soldiers a while ago. There was rice wrapped in the rising sun flag and some inner lids of mess kits on the floor. I set a fire and prepared supper. Then we slept under a roof for the first time in days.

The scorching sunlight in the southern country awoke me. I felt better because I slept well.

A mountain path, which only a small person could pass, continued to wind its way toward the northeast. There was no man, but the sun was shining, birds singing, and the heat haze was shimmering in the distance. It was the atmosphere of peaceful countryside, which made me forget the war. But I knew I had strayed from the main force, and I felt as if something rushed me, so I walked faster.

Then we walked north for several days, crossing mountains and rivers and descending gorges. However we couldn't get to the main road easily.

We found around 500g of rice on the way, which Japanese soldiers must have left, so we were not short of food. But, we ate rice without side dishes, soaked in the rain and dried, so we became weaker and weaker.

Wet clothes caused skin ulcers on my legs.

同年兵で背の高い朝長君が一番早く弱り、1 里も歩くとへたばってしまい皆で早く早くとしかりつけ、はげまし合って歩を進める。

途中また大きな河に出くわした。河幅は 50 メートルくらいで流れは速かったが、一ヵ所堤防の様な所があり、膝くらいの水位で、杖を頼りに足をすくわれそうになるのを踏みしめながら渡り終えた。

小さな部落が森蔭にあり友軍が 300 人くらい駐屯していた。そこで一泊し、翌日部隊と共に出発す。馬が数頭と砲が 1、2 門あり心強く感じたけれど、ある日大きな谷に遭遇して馬は谷をおりる事が出来ず、無理におろそうと隊長殿は声をからして兵を叱咤激励していたが、馬は谷をおりようとして足を折るやら、ころげるやらでとうとう殺して肉にしてしまった。我々も肉をと思ってかけよったが、はり倒された。

「お前等にやる肉はない。早く立ち去れ」

やむなく部隊が出発するのを見送り、骨に付いた肉を少しずつはがして取る。

朝長君がまた熱を出したのでそこで一泊する。朝起きてふと谷あいの細い道々に目を落とすと、アメリカ兵らしき者が 50 人くらい通っている。腰の「手榴弾」をにぎる。背中がゾクっとする。棒立ちのまま見送る。

皆を起こし、「ここは危険だ。早く行こう」と逃げる様にして谷をおり山を登る。

Mr. Tomonaga, a tall fellow soldier, was exhausted. He was too weak to continue walking over 4 km. We encouraged him to walk.

We came across a big river again. It was 50 meters wide, and flowing fast. One place was like an embankment, and the water level was knee-high. We managed to cross, trying to stand firm with a cane so that we wouldn't be swept away.

Around 300 Japanese soldiers were stationed in a small forest village. We stayed one night, and left with them the next day. Their horses and cannons reassured me. One day we encountered a ravine and the horses couldn't get down it. The captain encouraged his soldiers hoarsely to force the horses down. The horses fell down the ravine and broke their legs. They killed the horses to get meat. We ran up to get it, but they knocked us down. "There's no meat for you. Go away."

We had no choice but to obey. After the soldiers left, we peeled off the meat from the bones little by little.

Tomonaga got a fever again, so we stayed there overnight. Casually I looked down at the ravine after getting up the next morning. I noticed about 50 soldiers who appeared to be Americans passing along a path. I grasped the "grenade" at my waist. A shiver ran down my back. Standing still, I watched them until they were out of sight.

I woke everyone up and said, "It's dangerous here. Let's leave in a hurry." We hurried down the ravine and climbed a hill, feeling like we were running away.

その晩は大雨で真暗闇。一歩も進むことが出来ず雨に濡れながら寝る。

翌日、山を下り平坦地に出る。朝長君は疲れ果てて歩がおそいので少し早めに出発させる。休み休み歩を進め、夕暮近くやっと本街道に出る。本街道と言っても山を切開いた様な所で左は山、右は谷の様な感じの所だ。

ふと気が付くと先に歩いていた朝長君の姿が見えない、皆で手分けして捜すが見つからず、道は一本道だからその内先に行ったか、後から来るか、どこかで会うだろうと皆で話しながら前進する。

レストハウス近く、本街道に出る間際の山中で朝長君の姿を見うしない、その後、今日まで再び相まみえることはなかった。

1日でも半日でも草かげで休憩して朝長君の疲労をやわらげていたらと想ったり、しかしその時点ではまだ山中で本街道には出ておらず自分達の現在地も定かでない時で、一ときの駐留は同行の全員の死につながることと思い断念し強行した。

朝長君の冥福を祈ります。

1時間も歩いたと思われる頃、左手に登る小道に第百三十九兵站病院と書いた立札が目に付く。皆顔見合わせて喜び登る。竹やぶの中に小屋が見え、鶏が2、3羽いた。そうこうしている内に山の中は日の落ちるのが早いのか暗くなった。

It was heavy rain and dark that night. We couldn't move even a step forward, so we slept wet in the rain.

The next day, we went down the hill and onto a flat area. I let Tomonaga leave earlier because he was exhausted and walked slowly. Resting frequently, we moved forward. Finally, we came to the main road toward dusk. It was the main road, but it was like cutting through a mountain. The left side of the road was a mountain, and the right side was a ravine.

Suddenly I noticed that I had lost sight of Tomonaga, walking ahead. We searched for him, but couldn't find him. We moved forward, saying, "The road runs without branching. He may have gone ahead or will come later so we can meet him somewhere."

We lost sight of Tomonaga in the mountains near Rest-House just before the main road. I have not seen him again.

I wished we could have rested in the shade for a day or half a day to relieve his fatigue. We were still in the mountains without reaching the main road, and we weren't sure where we were. I was afraid that a short rest could lead to death of all members, and I was forced to proceed.

I pray for the repose of Tomonaga.

Walking for about an hour, I saw a bulletin board that said "139th Logistics Hospital" on the left side of the uphill path.

Looking at each other, we went up there with joy. We saw a shed with a few chickens in a bamboo thicket. It had already darkened, probably because the sun sets earlier in the mountains.

小屋の中には毛布が山の様にあり、毛布の山の上に身を横たえる。明日は鶏を料理して食おうやと話しながら眠る。

夜中砲弾の炸烈する音に飛び起きる。敵の迫撃砲弾が竹に当たり山にこだまし、次々に一定の間かくで炸裂する。本街道に出る500メートル位先に、道を中心に左右に激しく炸裂している。

瞬間身動きが出来ない。

落下点は規則正しく同じ様な場所に同じ様な間隔で落下炸裂している。落下点近くまで行き間隙を一気に走ろうと決め待機する。それ今だ、一生懸命かけ出す。次の落下の爆風で5メートル位吹きとばされ地面にたたきつけられたが、皆無事であった。

友軍は皆どこに行ったのか人影すら見当らず、迫撃砲は我々の頭上をシューンと音を立てて飛ぶ。

Many blankets were piled in the shed, and we lay on them. We went to sleep while talking about cooking and eating chicken tomorrow.

At midnight, we leaped to our feet at the sound of explosions. The enemy's mortar shells hit bamboo and echoed around the mountains. The shells exploded one after another at regular intervals. About 500 meters toward the main road, they exploded on both sides of the road.

We couldn't move for a moment.

The shells fell and exploded in similar places regularly. We decided to get close to the impact point, and run through the gap at once.

"Now is the chance. Go!"

We dashed as fast as we could. The next blast blew us five meters and knocked us to the ground, but everyone was safe.

I wondered where the Japanese soldiers had gone? Mortars whizzed over our heads.

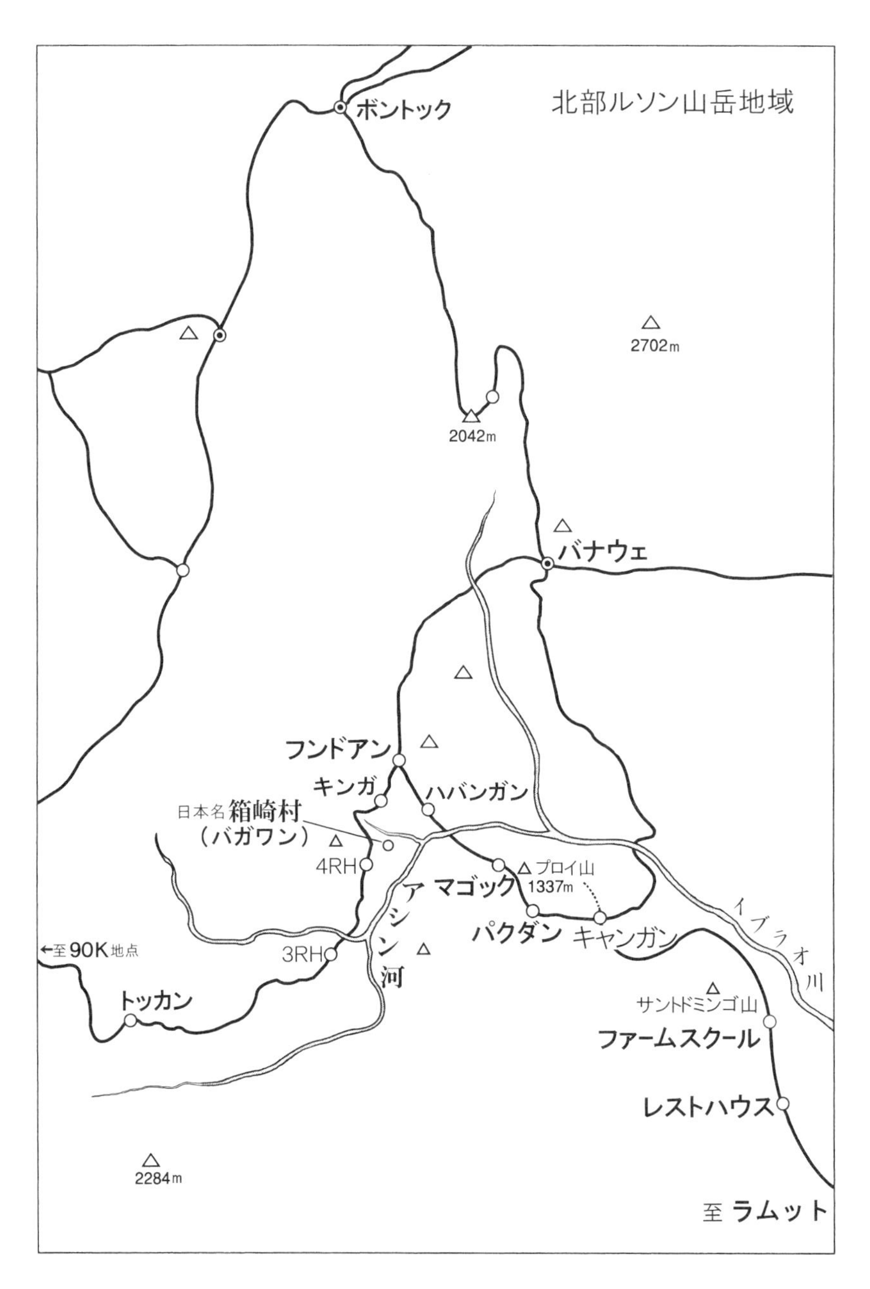
北部ルソン山岳地域
ボントック
2702m
2042m
バナウェ
フンドアン
キンガ
ハバンガン
日本名箱崎村
（バガワン）
4RH
マゴック
プロイ山
1337m
ア
シ
ン
河
パクダン
キャンガン
イブラオ川
←至90K地点
3RH
トッカン
サントドミンゴ山
ファームスクール
レストハウス
2284m
至 ラムット

Northwestern mountainous resion in Luzon

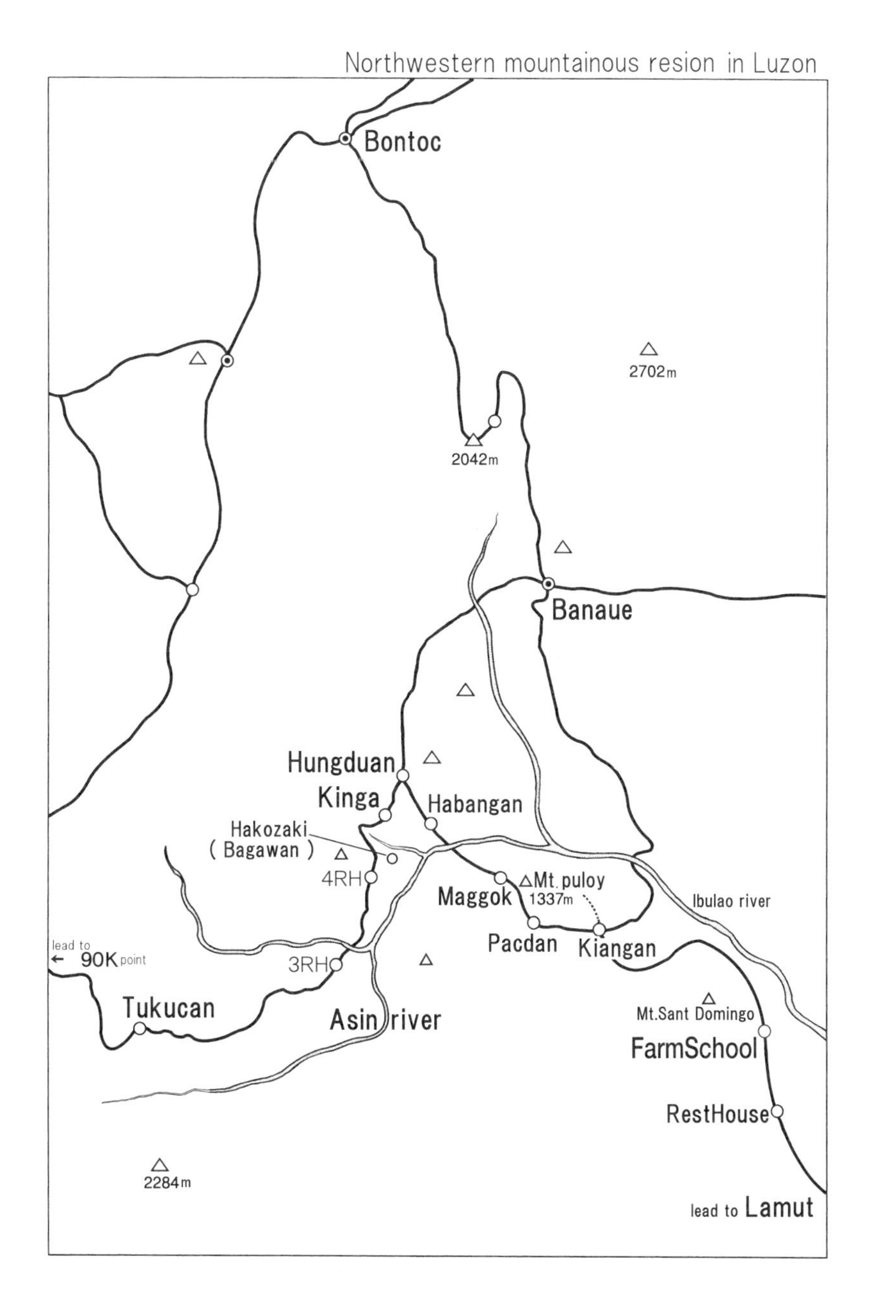

夜道をとぼとぼ声もなく歩く。

迫撃砲の音も聞こえなくなる。我々は敵の真ん中に居るのではないだろうか。昼は眠り夜は歩く、食糧も段々欠乏してくる。

数日後（日数の記憶も段々薄らぐ）、キャンガンに近づく。菊水隊と言う切込隊に会うがあまり元気がなさそうだ。時々前方より５、６人の兵が来る。どこへ行くかと聞けばファームスクールに食糧をとりに行くとの事だ。

キャンガンにたどりついたが本隊は出発のあと、休む間もなく歩く。雨は降る、道は暗く山道をおそるおそる進む。雨の中、峠のまがり角で草の中にたおれる様に眠る。思えば雨にたたかれながら良く眠れたものと思う。

人声に目をさます。目をさましてびっくり、我々はサントドミンゴ峠の山腹をけずり取った山道の絶壁のこぶの様に突出した岩の上に寝ている。下は千じんの谷底とも言われようか、アシン川の河原になっている。河原には大勢の軍が屯している。

山側には、雨上りのどんより曇った中に棒を立て毛布を天幕の様に張り、3、4 人の兵や在留邦人がいた。岩の上を息を殺して降り、また進む。干肉の 10 片ほど大事そうに干している女の人や、傷ついた兵がうつろな目をしてぼんやり座っているのやら、悪魔の羽根の中に包まれた様な雰囲気だ。

We trudged without a word in the night. The sound of mortars faded. I was afraid we might be in the middle of the enemy. We slept during the daytime and walked at night. Food was gradually running short.

Several days later — my memory for figures was getting worse — we came near Kiangan. I met a shock unit called Kikusui Unit, but they didn't look energetic. A group of 4 or 5 soldiers occasionally came from the front direction. When I asked where they were going, they said, "to Farm-School to get food."

We reached Kiangan, but the main force had left. We continued walking without rest. It rained. We went along a mountain path in the dark cautiously. We threw ourselves on the grass to sleep in the rain at the corner of a pass. Now I imagine I could sleep well, even being hit by the rain.

Voices woke me up. I was surprised that we were lying on a rock that juts out like a hump on a cliff by the mountain path of the St. Domingo Pass. It was a deep gorge, and the bottom was a riverbed of the Asin River. Many soldiers and people were staying there.

They spread blankets like tents on standing poles near the mountainside, overcast after the rain. Groups of 3 or 4 soldiers or Japanese residents were using each tent. We climbed down the rock carefully and proceeded again. A woman made ten pieces of dried meat, and some wounded soldiers sat in a daze with empty eyes. The atmosphere was as if they were in devil's wings.

つり橋を渡り、どこをどう通ったのか分からないがただ歩くのみ、我々の食糧もなくなり飢と言う事を少しずつ味わってくる。道には無数の死骸が腐臭を放って転っている様になる。どこの誰やら分らず。

我々はまだまだ元気であった。マラリアにもかからず、サツマ芋畑を見つけなんとか毎日食べていた。

パクダンに着くも本隊なし、教会が立っていた。天気が良く晴れ渡った朝だ、米を見つける。草むらの中に昼寝する。

ガサガサ音がするので眼をさますと目の前にイゴロット族が槍を持って立っている。やられたと思う。

よく見ると、頭のバラ籠にふかし立ての、サツマ芋と里芋を混ぜた様な味のする芋（カモテカホイと私達は呼んでいた）を乗せ、私達の腹にまいているネルの腹巻と交換してくれと手まねで言っている。交換して腹一杯食らう。

毎日腹一杯食べている様だが栄養不充分で、山道を登る時なかなか進まなくなる。若さのせいか楽天的なのか、または少しぼけていたのか、何の心配もなく、ただ本隊を目ざして毎日毎日トボトボと歩き続けていた。

あてどもなく山中を北へ向かって、さまよい歩き、雨に濡れ陽に照干され野宿しながら１ヵ月あまり。精神的苦痛は、部隊の迷子になっている事。肉体的疲労は如何ともし難い。

We crossed a suspension bridge, then just walked, not knowing where and how we passed. Our food was short, and I realized gradually what starvation was. Countless corpses were giving off a putrid smell as we passed. No one knew who the bodies were.

We were still alive. We found a sweet potato field and managed to live on it every day without suffering from malaria.

When we reached Pacdan, the main force was not there. There was a church. It was a sunny morning. We found some rice. We took a nap on the grass.

Something rustling woke me up. I found some Igorots standing with spears in front of me. I was afraid they would kill me!

Looking carefully, they had baskets of freshly puffed Cassava potatoes on their heads. I understood they were trying to say something with gestures. They wanted to exchange their Cassava for our belly supporters.

Deal! We ate our fill. It tasted like a sweet potato and taro mixture, and we called it Kamotekahoi.

I thought I ate enough every day. Poor nutrition made it hard for me to walk fast when I climbed a mountain path. I continued trudging daily to follow the main force without worry because I was young, optimistic, or dazed.

We were wandering the hills toward the north for one month, soaking in rain, drying in the sun, and sleeping outdoors. We were nervous that we had strayed from the main force. I couldn't help my physical fatigue.

毎日敵の迫撃砲の砲弾はシューン、シューンと不気味な音を立て頭の上をとんでいた。敵飛行機も毎日飛んでいたが、私達は眼中にない。

レストハウス、キャンガン、パクダンと部隊の足跡を辿り、アシン河の河原で休憩、吊橋を恐る恐る渡り、野に伏し山を登り、道端に木を削り第百三十九兵站病院入口と書いた標識を見た時は、皆、へなへなと座り込んでしまった。

安らぎと同時に、朝長君の疲れ果ててトボトボと歩く後ろ姿が目に浮んで涙が出て来た。アリタオを出発してから何日たったろうか、7月の17日ころと思う。

アシン河の河岸に点々とする部落の一つに本隊はいた。教育隊に報告する。

山田曹長に申告し、「良く生きていた」と喜んでくれた。行方不明(戦死)となっていた。

戦友に会う。「もう食糧も無し、毎日食糧を見つけるのが日課」と言っていた。

夜間、敵陣に迷い込んだり（すぐに気づいて引返す）、何度か「危険」に近づいたが、ゲリラに遭遇する事もなく、箱崎村（バガワン）の１３９兵站病院開設地に帰隊出来た事は御先祖様のお加護によるものと感謝している。

翌日、河で水浴をする。

The mortar shells were whizzing over our heads with an eerie sound every day. The enemy airplanes flew, but we were beneath their notice.

From Rest-House, to Kiangan, and to Pacdan, we followed the main force's tracks. We rested by the Asin riverside, crossed a rope bridge carefully, slept in the open, and climbed the hills.

When we saw a sign engraved on a tree showing the 139th logistics hospital entrance, we fell in a heap.

I felt relieved, but I remembered Tomonaga plodding in front of us, exhausted. Tears were coming to my eyes. How many days had passed since we left Aritao? I think it was July 17.

The main force was in one of the villages that dotted the Asin riverside. I reported our arrival to the training unit. Sergeant Major Yamada said, "I'm pleased you're alive." I had been considered missing or dead in the war.

I met one of my fellow soldiers. He said, "There's no food left. Finding food is our daily work."

We strayed into an enemy's camp in the night, but noticed immediately and turned back. Thus we were exposed to danger several times. We didn't encounter guerrillas. I am grateful to my ancestors that I was able to reach the 139th logistics hospital, which opened in Hakozaki village (the former name was Bagawan).

The next day, I bathed in the river.

9　第六患者輸送隊 さらなる苦労の始まり

落ち着く間もなく、7月20日、第六患者輸送隊へ矢上の樋口上等兵と転属を命ぜられる。

出発の際、病人だけいる小屋に行き、長崎の山下君に面会す。「元気で長崎に帰ろうよ」と話す。

昼過ぎ、島原士官殿に引率されて出発する。私の苦労はここから始まった。

患者輸送隊は本隊から4キロ位の前方におり、部隊長に報告する。後に丘をひかえ、前は谷のように下り段々畠が続いている。家の前は檳榔樹の林になっていた。家が20軒ほど横列に立ち並び、兵が入っていた。原住民は一人も見当らない。何万という日本軍が入り込んだので皆山の中に逃げ込んでいるのだろう。

翌日から毎日毎日パクダンまで米を取りに往復する。山を登り谷をすべりイゴロット族の槍を枕に夜はつかれ果て食欲もなく眠る。このままでは歩きながら死ぬのではないかと思う。

背嚢をせおって籾を一杯入れ帰り、また行く。靴は駄目になり素足で歩く。

(持ち帰った籾は誰が食べるのか？ 私達は芋を2、3個。これではたまらん、このまま死んだ方がましだ) と、やけ気味になる。

9 The 6th Patient Transport Unit ; Beginning of further hardships

Soon, PFC Higuchi and I were ordered to transfer to the 6th Patient Transport Unit on July 20. Before departing, I went to a sick person's hut to meet Yamashita from Nagasaki. I told him, "Let's return to Nagasaki safe and sound."

We left in the afternoon, led by Officer Shimabara. My hardships began here.

The 6th Patient Transport Unit was 4 km ahead of the main force. I reported my arrival to the commanding officer. There was a hill behind us, and a slope of terraced fields spread ahead. Groves of betel palms were in front of the houses. There were about 20 houses in a row, and Japanese soldiers occupied them. No native inhabitants were found. They fled into the mountains as tens of thousands of Japancsc troops entered the area.

From the next day, I made round trips to Pacdan to get rice. I climbed the hills and slid down the slopes. Using a spear of the Igorot tribe as a pillow, I was exhausted and slept with no appetite at night. If this situation continued, I might die while walking. I went back and forth, carrying a backpack full of rice in the husk. My shoes were worn out, so I had to walk barefoot.

"Who will eat the rice I brought? A few cassava for us. I couldn't stand it. I would rather die." I said to myself out of desperation.

山の草むら、川の渕に行倒れ、死んでいる日本兵の姿を見ると、
（こんな所で病気や飢えで一人ぼっちで死ぬのは御免だ。）

部隊はイゴロット族の家を使って駐屯していた。毎晩迫撃砲弾が家を越え谷間に炸裂していたが別に気にもならなかった。

8月上旬のある夜、私は夕方より寒気がして火をたいて毛布にくるまりふるえていた。

私達の小屋は部隊長、軍医殿、班長、樋口上等兵と私で本部と言う事らしい。部隊長は少佐殿で京大の出身とかで軍人らしからぬ物腰のやさしい人だった。イゴロット族の小屋は内地で良く見る寺の釣鐘堂のような所で、下は土間で2階は板ばりで四畳半くらい。

部隊長は私に、「今夜は上に寝ろ」と言われたが断わり、土の上に毛布を敷いて眠る。4、5日前より砲弾が家を越え田の中に毎日落下していた。部隊長殿は夜おそくまで下にいたが、虫の知らせか故郷の話などされ詩を吟じたりして機嫌良く上に登り眠りに就かれた。

夜半3時頃、砲弾が家の前のビンロー樹に当り、我々の小屋の上の部分、右左の小屋の部分を爆破した。ブワーッと熱風が体を包んだと思うと、目の前に真赤な光が走り思わず飛び起きた。樋口上等兵殿も私と一緒にいた。

上の部分にいた隊長は血達磨になって「助けてくれ」と言いながらズルズルとすべる様に下に落ちて来た。

When I saw dead Japanese soldiers on the grass on the hills or riverside, I thought, “I don’t want to die alone in such a place, sick or starving.”

The unit was stationed in the Igorots’ houses. Mortar shells were flying over our heads and exploding in a gorge every night, but I did not care.

One night in early August, I had a chill since the evening, so I made a fire and wrapped myself in a blanket, trembling.

Our hut was the unit headquarters, consisting of the commanding officer, the army doctor, the leader, PFC Higuchi, and me. The commanding officer was a major who graduated from Kyoto University. He was a gentle person in demeanor, unlike the common military man. The Igorots’ hut was like a temple bell hall in Japan. The first floor was earthen, and the second floor of the 2.5-meter-square was wooden.

“Sleep upstairs tonight, ” the officer told me. However, I declined. I put a blanket on the ground and slept there. For 4 or 5 days, the mortar shells flew over our hut and exploded in the rice fields. The officer was on the first floor late at night. He told me about his hometown and recited a poem in a good mood, then went upstairs to sleep. It may have been a foreboding.

Around 3 a.m., a shell hit the betel palm in front of the house. It blasted the upper part of our hut and the huts on both sides. A red flash appeared before my eyes, and a hot wind wrapped my body. I got up and jumped to my feet. PFC Higuchi was with me.

The officer upstairs was sliding downstairs, covered with blood, saying, “Help me!”

2人で隊長を抱き起こしたがもう駄目でした。

他の班長等は即死だ。

1分もたたない内に小屋は燃え上り、隣もまたその隣も。小銃弾や手榴弾に火が付きバンバンはじける。

「浜辺逃げろ」上等兵殿と2人で火の中を飛出し夢中になって走る。30秒くらい走って火の手の廻らない所まで行き退避する。上等兵殿は一度引きかえし食糧をみつけてくる。

夜が明け現場に行って見ると小屋は全部焼け落ち、黒こげの死体が5体まだ焼けていた。隊長もこの中におられた。右と左の小屋は下の人が即死、私達の小屋は上の人が即死、我々は九死に一生を得たことになる。

隊長等の死体の始末をして、午後、他の場所をもとめて出発する。どこに行くのやら私達には不明。装具も弾薬も食糧も何一つ残っていない。

マニラ陸軍病院より来た軍医中尉殿と私と樋口上等兵、班長と4人、他に兵が数名山道を歩く。

道端の溝の様な所に一人の兵がうずくまっていた。何となく気になってのぞいて見たらムニオス時代の戦友の堀口君だ。

「オィ、堀口」と呼んでもうつろな目を向けている。マラリアか赤痢にかかっているらしく、便のたれ流しか腰部は濡れベトベトしている。ただ食物を求めている様な目付きで私に手を出す。私も食べる物は何一つ持っていない。何故こんな所に堀口君はいるのだろ。

We held him up in our arms, but he was already dead.

Other leaders had died instantly. The huts flared up one after another within a minute. The bullets and grenades caught fire, blasting fiercely.

"Run away! Hamabe."

The PFC and I rushed out of the fire and ran desperately. Running for about 30 seconds, we took shelter without flames. The PFC returned once and brought food.

When we returned after dawn, I saw all the huts burned down, and five charred corpses were still burning. The commanding officer was among them. In the huts on both sides, the men on the first floor died instantly. In our hut, the man on the upper floor died instantly. We knew we had had a narrow escape.

After we buried the corpses, we left for another place in the afternoon. I didn't know where to go. We had few outfits, ammunition, and food. A first lieutenant army doctor from Manila Army Hospital, a sergeant, PFC Higuchi, some soldiers, and I walked along a mountain path.

A soldier was crouching in a place like a ditch by the roadside. Concerned somehow, I looked closely at him and found that he was my fellow soldier, Private Horiguchi, in Muñoz.

I said, "Hey! Horiguchi." But he saw me with blank eyes. He seemed to be suffering from malaria or dysentery. Because of stool incontinence, his lower back was wet and sticky. He held out his hand at me with eyes that seemed to demand food. I had no food at all. Why was Horiguchi in such a place?

「頑張れよ」ただそれしか言えない。

本隊の居る所まで来た。この坂の下に多くの戦友がいるのになあと思いながら後方にさがる。

これ以上進むのは無理と想われる様なアシン河の上流の一部落に落着く。

それからは食糧探しに出かける日々だった。

毎日毎日食糧をもとめてさまよう日々が続く。道には兵隊や邦人の死がいがころがっている。

敵機はゆうゆうと飛んで来ては爆弾を落して行く。時にはガソリンを落し焼夷弾を投下し一山燃えつくす様な事までやり出す。1ヵ所に落ちつく事も出来ず、山の中へ中へと歩を進め小屋を見つける。中に入ると邦人の人々が枕をならべて骨になっているのに常に会う。

サツマ芋も掘りつくし葉も食べつくし、樋口上等兵と2人で毎日短剣ひとつ持って芋もない畠の中をウロウロして掘り残しの芋の新芽をもとめてさまよう。1日かかって2つか3つ軍医に食べさせる。

そのうち軍医に食べさせる芋も見つける事が出来なくなる。

ある日、葉の青々とした畠を見つける。その日は背のう一杯掘る事ができ大喜びで帰る。途中ヘビを1匹掴まえる事もでき、何日かぶりで肉を食べ芋も腹一杯食べて殿様になった様な気分で眠る。

What I could only say to him was, “Good luck.”

I came to where the main force was. I went backward, thinking that many comrades were under this slope.

We settled in a village in the upper reaches of the Asin River, where it seemed impossible for us to go further.

After that, we went looking for food day after day. We had to spend days wandering around searching for food. The corpses of Japanese soldiers and residents lay on the path.

The enemy’s planes sailed over and dropped bombs. Sometimes, they burned the entire mountain by dropping gasoline and incendiary bombs. We couldn’t settle down in one place, so we kept walking deeper into the hills until we found a hut. Whenever we entered the huts, we saw Japanese residents’ bones arranged side by side.

We ate up all the sweet potatoes and their leaves. Higuchi and I wandered with a dagger around the fields with no sweet potatoes, expecting to find sprouts every day. We got two or three potatoes a day and gave them to the army doctor. Soon, we couldn’t find any sweet potatoes for the army doctor.

One day, I found a potato field covered with lush foliage. I filled my backpack with them and returned in delight. On my way back, I caught a snake too. I ate enough meat and potatoes for the first time in many days and slept, feeling as if I were a feudal lord.

3日ほどしてまた掘りに行く。1日かかって掘り上げ帰路に就く途中、銃を持った友軍10人位に取りかこまれ芋を取り上げられる。

また何日か歩いて山深い一部落に着く。山と山がせり合う様にせまり段々畠が急斜面にならび、一番上に10軒ほどの小屋がある。

夕暮れも間近、薄暗く雨がシトシト降り出し、あえぎながら坂道を登って小屋の中に入り死んだ様に眠りこける。

毎日毎日が食糧をもとめてのさまよい歩き。手には、手榴弾2発とさびた剣一ふり、食物もなかなか手に入らない。1日さがして芋1つ2つ、水ばかりの日もあり、耳鳴りがして思考力もなくなり、食物の事ばかり。「畳の上で米の飯と豆腐の味噌汁を腹一杯食べたら死んでも良かね」と想った。

班長は1週間に1度ほど命令受領に行く。

Three days later, I went there again. I dug potatoes all day, but 10 Japanese soldiers surrounded me with guns on my way back. They robbed me of the potatoes.

After walking for several days, we reached a village deep in the mountains. The mountains rose high over us as if competing for the highest. We could see their steep slopes lined with terraced fields and about ten huts on the upper part.

It was toward dusk, dim, and began to drizzle. I climbed up the slope, panting, and entered the hut. I slept like a log.

I wandered around looking for food day after day with a rusty dagger and two grenades in my hand. It was tough to get food. I got one or two potatoes a day with sometimes nothing but water. I had a ringing in my ear and became unable to concentrate. I was thinking only of food. How happy I would be if I could sit on the tatami mats and eat full of rice and miso soup with tofu before dying!

The leader went to receive a command once a week.

10　8月15日と降伏

空襲もなく砲撃もなく、戦争の最中とは想えなく、何のために、こんな所に私達はいるのか。手榴弾が2発あるから、せめて米軍陣地まで行ってたたき込んで死んでやろうかなー。それにしても、8月15日から、やけに静かだ。

8月20日頃しびれを切らして途を逆行して見た。日本軍の兵士に会う。

「おいおい、お前はどこの部隊だ」　「ハイ輸送隊です」と言うと、その兵はそばによって来てポケットから紙片を出して見せてくれた。

日本軍全面無条件降伏の活字が目の中に飛込んで来た。

8月15日、敵空軍が終戦のビラを散布していたのだった。

「本当だろうか」「さあ分らんばい」何人かの兵が集まって来た。

「この前から空襲も砲撃もないから、戦いは終わったのかも、無条件降伏なんてあるものか」と、がやがや皆勝手な事を言っていたが、顔には皆安堵の色が浮かんでいた。

やれやれと思う。あと1ヵ月もすれば我々はみな餓死していた事だろう。半信半疑ながら敵機の姿も見えず戦争は終わったのかなあと思う様になる。

10 August 15, 1945, and the Surrender.

There was neither an air raid nor a bombardment. I couldn't imagine that we were in the midst of war. Why are we in such a place? I have two grenades, so I think I should try to at least go up to the US military base, throw them and die. But it was strange that it had been quiet since August 15.

I got impatient and turned back down the path on August 20. I met a Japanese soldier.

He asked me, "Hey, which unit do you belong to?"

"I'm in the patient transport unit, sir."

He came up to me, took a piece of paper out of his pocket, and showed it.

"The Japanese Army's unconditional surrender"

The enemy air force had distributed leaflets of the war's end on August 15.

"Is this true?"

"I don't know," said one of the soldiers gathered.

"There has been no air raid or bombardment for the last few days. So the war may be over. But it can't be unconditional surrender."

Everyone said what they liked, but looked relieved.

I sighed in relief. We would have starved to death if it had continued a month longer. There were no enemy planes, so I started to think the war was over, although I was half in doubt about it.

数日後、来た道を引返す。マゴックの十二陸軍病院に集合し、陸軍病院の指揮下に入る。

患者の50名ほどを90キロ地点まで輸送するので使役1名出せ、と私達樋口上等兵など5、6名集まっている所に命令が来た。
「浜辺、お前行け」　「ハイ」
最後の最後までこき使われる。（初年兵はつらいよなー）と腹で想う。
各小屋より1名出ることになり私が選ばれたのだ。
「1日4キロ、3日位の行程で途中食物は芋だが、若干用意しておるから」と言われた。
朝早く出発する。
米軍収容所の近くまで送り、また引返すのだ。50メートル進んでは休み、また進むが、何のことなく90キロ地点まで誰もいない。ましては食物など一片もなく、まただまされた。患者も私達もへとへと。90キロ地点に着いたのは日没近く夕闇が静かに立ちこめている時刻で、100メートル位先に白い天幕が見え、何かの旗が立っていた。
患者の中の上級者を呼び、
「自分達の任務はこれまでだから引返すので、貴方が引率してあの幕舎に入って下さい」と頼むと、コックリとうなづいたので引返す。往復とも食糧もなく10日ほど歩き続ける、歩くことが自分の運命の様に……。

A few days later, we returned the way we had come. We gathered at the 12th Army Hospital in Maggok and were under its command.

An order came to where five or six soldiers, including PFC Higuchi and I, had gathered. We should transport about 50 patients to the 90 km mark point and select one soldier in command.

"You should go, Hamabe." "Yes. sir!"

They have pushed me around to the bitter end.

I told myself, "Military life's hard on a recruit!"

Each hut was ordered to pick a leader, and they chose me from my hut.

"Walk 4 km a day. It'll take three days to reach the 90 km mark point, and we will prepare some sweet potatoes as food on the way."

We left early in the morning.

The command said we should send the patients near the US Army camp and return. We rested every 50 meters advance. But, nobody was on the way to the 90 km point, let alone a piece of food. I was tricked again. All the patients and I were exhausted. It was toward dusk when we arrived at the 90 km point. I saw a white tent and a flag standing about 100 meters ahead.

I called the senior patient and told him, "My mission is done, so I'll return. Please lead the patients to the camp."

He nodded, so I returned. I had walked for ten days without food both ways as if it was my destiny to walk.

途中、１３９兵站病院の山口上等兵が先頭で50名くらいの隊列が歩いて来るのに出会った。

出発地点まで帰って見たら、樋口上等兵たちはいない。私達は5、6名、指揮者なく取残された感じ。何故いつもこんな状態になるのかなー。もう10日あまり水しかのんでいない。

陸軍病院の兵は出発したあとで、他の部隊が10数人くらい残っていた。

「おい、浜辺ではないか」

と声をかけられ、立ち止まるとムニオス病院に入院して私が世話した事のある水谷曹長だった。

「曹長殿、何か食べる物はないですか」

「さっきまで芋が少しあったのだがなー。今は何もない。今からキャンガンの米軍陣地まで行く、浜辺達も一休みしたら出発しろよ。我々は一足先に行く」と、水谷曹長は部下と共に出発して行った。

私達も一休みして出発する。1日かかって1里も歩けるか歩けないかであった。

2、3日後、「浜辺、浜辺」と呼んでいる声が耳に入るが、なかなか体が前に進まない。敵機が落した食糧を水谷曹長の部下が谷底よりひろい上げて来たのを私に食べさせようと思って持って来てくれたのだ。

おしつぶされた缶詰を10個ほど頂く。ジャムやビスケット、ひき肉など私と同行した5人くらいの人々も手を出したが、

On the way, I met PFC Yamaguchi of the 139th Logistics Hospital, leading 50 soldiers.

I returned to the starting point to find no PFC Higuchi or anyone else. Five of us were left behind without a leader. Why did this always happen? I had had nothing but water for ten days.

The soldiers of the Army Hospital had already left. Ten soldiers of the other unit remained there.

I heard someone say, "Hey, aren't you Hamabe?" and stopped walking.

The man was Master Sergeant Mizutani, whom I had cared for in the hospital in Muñoz.

"Do you have anything to eat, master sergeant?"

"No. A few sweet potatoes were a while ago, but we don't have any food now. We're going to the US Army camp in Kiangan. You should leave after taking a rest. We'll go now." Master Sergeant Mizutani left with his soldiers.

We also took a break and left. We were able to walk only about 4 kilometers a day.

A few days later, I heard someone calling, "Hamabe, Hamabe!" But I had difficulty advancing. It was Master Sergeant Mizutani. He brought me some rations, dropped by US planes and picked up by his subordinate at the bottom of a ravine.

I received about ten crushed cans. There were jam, biscuits, ground meat, etc. Five soldiers accompanying me also held out their hands to get food.

「おれは浜辺に命を助けられているので浜辺にはどうしても食べさせなければならない。皆もやりたいが、部下が命がけで拾って来たのを自分も分けてもらったのだからかんべんしてくれ。では元気でな、私達はそこで野営する」

涙を流しながら砕けたビスケットを口に入れる。味もなんにも分からないながら食べる。缶を半分くらい食べたら、今まで10何日間何も食べていないので胃が受付けないのか、グアーッと吐き出す。

朝起きまたトボトボ歩く、本隊の駐屯していた地点を通る。(皆もう出発したのかなー。)

パクダンまでたどり着くと邦人の婦女子がいた。皆マラリアと赤痢にやられている。いつもらったのか記憶がないが私は腕に赤十字の腕章をはめていた。

集結した兵が100名くらいになっていた。衛生兵は私が一人である。兵をまとめ、在留邦人を担架で運ぶ事になる。

毛布で作った急造担架を4人で運び、うれしいことには地下足袋の新品を支給してくれ、文数も丁度良かった。

4人1組で担架を造り女性を乗せ山を下る。担ぐ兵が皆病人の様な状態なので乗っている人は助かり、担いだ兵は朝起こすとつめたくなっていると言う様なことをくり返しくり返し進む。

私の乗せていた人はマニラで大きな料理屋を経営していた女将だったが、栄養失調で体はむくみ見るかげもなくはれ上がっていた。

Master Sergeant said, "I owe my life to Hamabe in the hospital, so I must get Hamabe to eat at any cost. I wanted to give food to everybody, but my subordinate picked it up at the risk of his life and shared it with me. Forgive me. Well, take care. We'll encamp here."

I put the broken biscuits in my mouth, shedding tears. I ate them without tasting anything. When I ate half of them, I vomited because I had not eaten for over ten days.

The following day, I trudged again. I passed where the main force had been stationed.

"I wonder if everybody has already left."

When I reached Pacdan, there were Japanese women and children. All of them had malaria or dysentery. I wore the Red Cross armband, though I didn't remember when I had gotten it.

Around 100 soldiers gathered. Only I was a medical soldier. We decided to carry sick Japanese residents on stretchers. Four soldiers carried a makeshift stretcher made of a blanket. To my delight, they provided me with a new pair of Japanese shoes, fitted to me.

A group of four soldiers made a stretcher and carried a woman on it down the mountain. The soldiers were all mostly sick, so patients on the stretchers survived, but the soldiers who carried them died the next morning. That happened repeatedly while we were proceeding.

The woman I carried used to be an owner of a big restaurant in Manila. Because of malnutrition, she was swollen.

「すまない、すまない」と言いつづけながら、小休止の時小用をすると言うので、やぶかげに担架を入れ待機していたが、なかなか声がないので行って見たら死んでいた。

キャンガンに着くまでは何人もの人が、かつぐ人もかつがれる人も死んで行った。夜、小屋を見つけて寝ようとすると必ず小屋の中には白骨化した死体が枕を並べて死んでいた。一緒に死んで行ったのではないのに､最後の人が並べたのだろう。女の人だろうと思う、小屋の中で風がないので白骨化した頭がい骨の上に長い黒髪がかぶさっていた。黒髪の間から大きくあいた眼窩が見えて私に何か語りかけるような気がして、一瞬鬼気せまる感じで頭をふる。

＊　　　＊

キャンガンのアメリカ軍の近くまで来た。一面砲弾の跡の大きな穴があいていた。戦の激しかった事が偲ばれる。

毎日のように降る雨のため道は泥沼と化して足を取られ、動けない兵が数 10 人 もがいていた。

キャンガンの米軍陣地に着いた時、私は 7 歳くらいの男の子をおんぶしていた。

門の前で 1 人 1 人点検され武器は取られ、軍用食のレーションを 3 食分もらう。肉、煙草、ビスケット、チョコレートが入っている。あわてて食べて、ここまで生きて来たのに命を落とした兵も数多くあった。

She repeated, "Thank you, thank you." She asked to urinate during a brief rest, so we put the stretcher in a bush and waited. However, she didn't say anything even though time had passed. We went to find her dead.

Many people, those carrying and those being carried, died before reaching Kiangan.

Whenever I found a hut and went into it to sleep at night, skeletons were laid side by side. They couldn't have died at the same time, but I suppose that the last person may have lined them up. There was no wind in the hut, and long black hair covered the bleached skull. I thought it would be a woman. When I saw the eye sockets through the black hair, I felt she was telling me something. I felt frightened for a moment and turned my head away.

*　　　　*

I approached the U.S. Forces in Kiangan. All over the area, the shells had made many large holes. I could imagine how violent the battle had been.

It had been raining day after day, so dozens of soldiers stuck in the mud were struggling to get out.

When I reached the U.S. camp in Kiangan, I was carrying a seven-year-old boy on my back.

US soldiers checked each of us in front of the gate and took away our weapons. They gave us three military rations that contained meat, cigarettes, biscuits, and chocolate. Quite a lot of soldiers died eating in a hurry, though they had survived until then.

途中の道が崩壊しトラックがキャンガンまで来られないと言う事で、その夜、夜道をついて峠を越える。一晩歩き続け平野に出る。

小さな天幕を張った中に一日中照り続け焼けつく様な南国の太陽に灼かれながら汗を流し死んだように眠る。ひ弱な私が良くここまで命長らえたものだと感心する。

安心感と疲れが一度に出たのか、翌朝護送用のトラックが来た時には歩く事が出来なくなっていた。アメリカ兵に抱きかかえられトラックに乗る。

昭和 20 年 10 月初頭になっていた。

The road to Kiangan collapsed, and trucks couldn't get there, so we crossed the pass at night. We walked all night and came out on the plain.

Scorched by the sun's harsh glare all day long in the southern country, I was dead asleep sweating in a small tent. I was impressed that a weak frame like me was able to survive until then.

Because of relief and a surge of tiredness, I couldn't walk when escort trucks came the next morning. A US soldier carried me in his arms and made me get into the truck.

It was early October 1945.

11　収容所キャンプ

数ヵ月飢えにさいなまれ彷徨したアシン河の地獄谷に別れを告げ、やがてトラックは山岳地帯を離れカガヤン平野に出る。

バガバッグ、バンバン、アルマゲルの三叉路、アリタオ、サンタフェ、バレテ峠と向かうのだ。

バガバッグに入る頃、待ちかまえていたとばかりに比島人はトラックに向かって、「ドロボー、バカヤロー」と口々にさけんで石を投げつける。かつて日本軍が盛んな頃は家々に日の丸を立て、「バンザイ、バンザイ」と繰りかえしていたことを思えば、負けたことが今さらながら残念に思う。

バトー橋を渡りバンバンに入る。車の上から思い出しながら眺める。アリタオを過ぎバレテの峠に向かう。三世らしい比島人が4、5人通る。ここでもバ声をあびる。バレテのふもとは一面すすきが生え繁り白っぽい穂が私達の運命を悲しむ様になびいていた。

バレテ峠にさしかかった時は夕もやが立ち込め、もうすぐ暮れようとしている時刻だった。すすきの白い穂が風に揺れ何か物悲しい。家路を急ぐ比島人が三々五々通り、私達を見ると、
「バカヤロー、スケベー、ドロボー」
と、あらゆる憎言を発し、路端の石をつかんでボンボン投げつけ

11 The camp

We left the hell valley along the Asin River, where we had been wandering, tormented by starvation, for months. Soon, the truck left the mountain area and entered the Cagayan plains. It was going to Bagabag, Bambang, the 3-way junction of Almaguer, Aritao, Santa Fe, and Balete Pass.

When we entered Bagabag, Filipinos had been waiting for us. They threw stones at our truck, shouting, "Dorobo, Bakayaro!" When the Japanese Army was thriving, Filipinos raised the Rising Sun at their houses and called "Banzai, Banzai," many times. After all this time, it was regrettable that Japan lost the war.

After crossing the Batu Bridge, we entered Bambang. I looked around town from the truck, remembering what had happened there. Passing Aritao, we headed for Balete Pass. Several Filipinos, seemingly 3rd-generation Japanese Filipinos, were walking by us. They booed and jeered at us here again. At the foot of Balete Pass, Japanese pampas grass was growing thick over the area. Its whitish ears swayed as if they were feeling sad about our fate.

When we approached Balete Pass, it was toward dusk, and an evening haze hung all around us. White ears of Japanese pampas grass were swaying in the wind, which made us sad somehow. Filipinos rushing home by twos and threes saw us and hurled a torrent of abuse at us.

"Bakayaro, Sukebe, Dorobo." ("You fool, lecher, thief!")

They picked up stones and threw them at us. They did it

て来た。運転者の交替で、トラックを止めていたので益々激しく、警備で乗車していた米兵が、たまりかね銃口を空に向かって数発、発砲したら彼等は立去った。

牛車を引いてプンカンを出発した時は、この様な姿になろうとは夢にも思わなかった。サンホセからバレテ峠まで水牛を引いて１ヵ月余りかかって越えた山々は、生長の速いと思われる熱帯の木々も、砲弾の雨で皆黒く焼かれ、さがしてもさがしても緑の木を１本も見ることは出来なかった。夕やみも近く、砲爆撃でぶち切られ黒こげになった大木も骸骨のように見えて鬼気をも感じた。

撃兵団、鉄兵団が死守したと聞く。遠い異国の地で万こくのうらみを抱いて死んで行った戦友達よ、安らかに眠れ。

１月あまりかかった行程を、馬力の強いエンジンの米軍のトラックは暗闇の中を大きな音を立てながら走る。天幕もなくトラックの荷台に座っている。夜風が容赦なく肌を突きぬけ弱り果てた肉体には苦しい。皆うずくまって膝頭を抱くように体を丸くして無言でいた。

夜中にムニオスに着く。

１年余暮したムニオスの街を見ようと思ったが変わりはててどこがどこやら分らない。日本軍占領下には電気もなく椰子の油で夜をしのいでいたのが、今では電気が明々と灯り、ダンスホールでも出来ているのか、遠くからジャズの音が聞えて来ていた。

more violently because the truck had stopped for a driver's shift. A US soldier, onboard as a guard unable to watch, fired a few times into the sky, and they left.

When I left Puncan dragging a water buffalo, I never knew I would be in such a situation. It took more than a month from San Jose to Balete Pass with a buffalo in tow. Tropical trees, which seem to grow fast, were burned black by a rain of cannonballs. I couldn't see one green tree no matter how I looked around the mountains. It was toward dusk. Big trees, split and charred by bombardment, looked like skeletons. They made me feel ghastly.

I heard the divisions known as "Geki" and "Iron" had defended there to the death. May they rest in peace with their fallen comrades in a faraway land!

The high-powered US Army truck drove in the dark, making a loud noise. It was the same journey that had taken us over a month. I sat on the truck deck without a tent. The night wind pierced my skin and tormented my exhausted body. Everyone was crouching around silently and holding their knees.

We reached Muñoz late at night.

I looked at the town of Muñoz, where I had spent over a year. However, it had changed beyond my recognition. The Japanese army didn't provide electricity during the occupation. So, we used palm oil for light at night. But now, it was lit brightly. I heard jazz from a distance. Seemingly a dance hall had been built around there.

トラックから降ろされ、貨車に積込まれるように着剣した米兵にせきたてられる。貨車に乗せられマニラに向かって進む。

途中サンフェルナンドに停車。

「病人はおらんか」と通訳がどなる。「病人はここの病院に入れる」

皆知らない兵ばかりであったが、

「降りるな、降りるな、どげんなるか分らんぞ」と、病人も何人かいたが皆がまんして降りない。

マニラ近くで下車、トラックを待つ。「どうなるのかなー」こそこそ話し出す。

「ポツダム宣言の条文の中にＰＷはすみやかに本国に帰すと謳っているから、すぐマニラから船に乗るんだろう」なんて楽観していた。

トラックが来て乗る。しばらく進んだと思う頃、様々の服装をした人々が何百人となくゾロゾロ歩いている。

「あれはなんだろう」異様な気持でいた。近づくに従いますますおかしい、日本人に見える。

「オーイ」と向こうの人達がさけび、手をふっていた。おれ達もああなるのだ、すぐ帰れると楽観していた気分も空気の抜けた風船のようにしぼむ。マニラから直ぐ船に乗ると思っていたのに……。

バリケードの囲いの中に一人一人入れられ、真っ裸になる。四方よりＤＤＴをふりかけられる。出口では米兵が立っていて一人一人にシャツとパンツを渡してくれた。

A US soldier with a sword ordered us to get off the truck and rush to get on a freight train. The train was headed toward Manila.

It stopped at San Fernando on the way.

"Are there any sick guys?" an interpreter shouted. "We'll let the sick guys go into the hospital here."

All the soldiers were strangers to me.

One said, "Don't get off, don't get off. There's no telling what'll happen to us."

Some were sick, but nobody dared get off.

We got off the train near Manila and waited for our trucks.

"What'll happen to us?" someone whispered.

"The Potsdam Declaration provisions stipulate prisoners of war are to be promptly repatriated, so we'll soon get on a ship at Manila." We were optimistic.

A truck arrived, and we got on. Driving for a while, we saw hundreds of people walking wearing various clothes.

"What are they?" I felt strange. As I approached them, I felt even more bizarre. They looked Japanese.

"Hey!" they shouted in Japanese, waving their hands.

"We'll become like those people." The bright idea of returning to Japan had shrunk like a deflated balloon. I had hoped to get on a ship as soon as we arrived at Manila.

They put each of us in a barricade fence and forced us to strip naked, and sprinkled DDT from every direction. US soldiers stood at the exit and gave each of us underwear.

幕舎に入る。キャンガン出発以来、食糧は配給されていない。私達の着ていた物は皆焼却していた。伝染病予防のためだ。

夕方一食分のレーション（携帯食糧）をもらう、周囲は知らない兵ばかりだったが、4、5日すると馴れて色々と話し合う様になる。6日目に米兵が来て牛蒡抜きにあちらこちらから連れ出し、またトラックに乗せられ、山すその名前も分らないキャンプに連行される。その様な事が数回くり返された。

私達と一緒に貨車に乗せられ収容所に運ばれた兵の中に手榴弾を隠し持ち、キャンプを爆破しようとした兵がいたと言うことで目を付けられていたらしい。

とにもかくにも、日がたつにつれてキャンプの整備もととのい、炊事場も出来、米の飯とは行かないが、飯粒が数粒泳いでいるスープを朝夕米軍食器に一杯出るようになる。一息で飲み干す。空腹は山の中よりひどい。

靴の配給があった。米軍の軍靴は脚絆付だ。足を入れたが靴が重くて足があがらない。見渡せば学校の理科室にある骸骨の標本のようで、関節が大きく見え、腰骨などは見られた姿ではない。まるで、骨の上に皮がついた標本だ。

このやせおとろえて肉のない下半身に意地悪く、山中で患った南方潰瘍が身をむしばみ、痒くてたまらない。

We entered the camp lodge. They haven't distributed any food to us since we left Kiangan. They burned everything we were wearing to prevent infectious disease.

In the evening, we were given rations. The soldiers around me were strangers, but we got used to each other after four or five days and talked about things.

On the 6th day, US soldiers came and picked out each of us at random. They made us get on a truck and took us to another camp at the foot of a mountain. They repeated these things several times.

One soldier taken to the camp with us by the same train had tried to blow up the base, holding a concealed grenade. They seemed to place us on a watch list.

Anyway, as the days passed, they equipped the camp and built a kitchen. They served us soup with a bit of rice floating in it morning and evening. The dishes were US Army tableware. I ate it in a moment. The hunger was worse than in the mountains.

They distributed shoes to each of us. The US military shoes were leggings, too heavy for me to lift my feet. When I looked at people around, they were like specimens of skeletons in a school science room. The joints stood out, and the hipbones looked awful. We were like specimens with skin on their bones.

A skin disease, which I had suffered from in the mountains, affected the emaciated lower part of my body. It was itchy.

第一キャンプの医務室に午前中に入って薬を塗ってもらう。何10人と来ていた。薬と言ってもわけの分らない、スタンプインキのように青い液体を羽毛でベタベタ塗ってくれる。米兵は面白がって塗らないで良い所にも塗る、乾くと夜光虫の様な色になる。

空腹は相変らず農園の使役で実っている「なま」の豆をかじる。自動車工場などの使役にも出るようになり、米軍も段々友好的になって来た。

ある日キャンプの正門に庭園を造ると言うことで、50人くらい着剣した米兵に護られ近くの河に石を取りに行く。途中砂糖きび畠があった。最初は歩きながら、米兵の目をぬすんで走りより手折って、かじっていたが、監視の米兵もきび畠の監視所のようなやぐらに昇り昼寝をしていた。私達は無我夢中で甘い汁をむさぼり吸いつく。

米兵が目をさました時は、皆きび畠の中に潜入していて姿が見えなくなっていた。あわてて怒り、銃を発砲する。銃声に驚いて路に這いもどり整列する。

河で石を一つずつ各人に持たせ「ハバハバ」と走らせた。靴をはいて足が上がらない体力に石を持って走る事が出来ましょうか。頭に来た米兵は竹の鞭でたたく。比島の竹の枝にはトゲがある。裸の体を鞭でたたかれ、トゲで血を出し、夜中頃キャンプに帰る。

I went to the first camp infirmary in the morning to have some medicine applied. Dozens of patients were there. US soldiers applied ink like blue liquid, an unknown ingredient, using a feather. They put it on the unnecessary part for fun. When it was dry, it became Noctiluca's color.

I was as hungry as ever. I gnawed raw beans that were growing while working on the farm. Sometimes I went to work at a car factory. US soldiers gradually became friendly toward me.

One day, it was decided to build a garden at the camp's main gate. Nearly 50 people and I, escorted by an armed US soldier, went to a nearby river to get stones. There was a sugarcane field on the way. At first, we approached the sugarcanes secretly while walking, broke, and nibbled them. Later, we devoured sweet juice because the US soldier was taking a nap in a place like a lookout post.

When he woke up, he couldn't find us because we had hidden in a sugarcane field. He got upset, became angry, and fired his gun. Surprised at the shot, we headed back to the road and lined up.

Saying, "Hubba, Hubba!" he made each of us pick up a stone from the river and run with it, but I couldn't. I was so weak that I couldn't even raise my legs wearing heavy US Army shoes. The angry US soldier beat me with a bamboo rod. A bamboo branch in the Philippines is thorny. He whipped my naked body. I returned to the camp late at night, bleeding from my skin.

キャンプ全員晩飯は絶食だった。

米兵の中にも友好的な人もいたが、昨日まで敵であった私達だ、いい顔は出来ないでしょう。特に今次大戦で肉親をうしなった人は殊更に。

11 月の末近くなると食料も「オモユ」から「お粥」になった。若干腹に入った感じだった。いろんな使役も悪くはなくなった。

時々、全員整列、一列横隊。なんだろうと話し合っていると、米軍将校、兵などと、比島人が数人来て、比島人が私達一人一人の顔を丹念に穴のあくほど睨みつけ見て回った。加藤とか鈴木とかの姓の人は全員呼ばれたりしていた。

日本軍に悪いことをされた比島人が、顔を見ていたり、呼び合った時の姓名をおぼえていたりして、そのうらみをはらさんがため来るのだそうな。それを聞いてから、首実検の際は顔をそむけるようにする。別にうらみを受けるようなことはしていないけど、間違って「これだ」と言われたらと思うと身が震える。

12 月に入った頃。米軍の中に日系人二世で、米国籍を持って将校になっている人も多くいるとのこと。そのような将校より個々に呼ばれ、入隊時から現在までの行動について色々と尋問された。その後数回同じことを尋問された。尋問する将校はそのたび違う人だった。

Dinner wasn't served to anyone at the camp.

Some US soldiers were friendly. However, others were not, especially those who lost their families in World War II. After all, we had been their enemies until the day before.

In late November, food changed from "thin rice gruel" to "rice gruel". I felt less hungry. I began to feel the various kinds of labor were not so bad.

"Everybody, line up in a straight line!" Sometimes they commanded us. U.S. Army officer, US soldiers, and several Filipinos came when we were wondering what was going on. They walked around, scrutinizing each of our faces. They picked out people by their surnames such as Kato or Suzuki.

I heard that some Filipinos, whom Japanese soldiers had oppressed, were there to get revenge. They remembered the Japanese soldiers' faces, or names when they heard them called.

After learning their purpose, I tried to turn my face away during identification. I had never done anything to earn their hatred, but I was afraid they could accidentally call my name. That would be terrible.

It was the beginning of December. In the U.S. Army, quite a few Japanese Nisei with US citizenship served as officers. Those officers asked each of us many questions about what we had done since joining the army. Then they asked me the same thing several times. The officer who interrogated was different each time.

第一キャンプに移る別枠のバリケードの中に山下将軍がいたとか、いるとかと話していたのを聞いたが、何の感情もわかない。
第六輸送隊に転属になって以来、139 兵站病院の戦友には会っていない。唯一人同年兵の堀口君に道端で移動中会っただけだったので、139 兵站病院の戦友達の消息が気になっていた。

12 月に入ると帰国者の名簿がマイクでキャンプの本部から発表され出した。幕舎中の人間がその時間には本部前に集まってジーッと耳をすまし、固唾をのんで、やせ細った足を抱くような姿勢でいた。名前を呼ばれた者は表現の仕様のない様な顔をしていた。呼ばれなかった者は肩を落しトボトボと幕舎に帰る。

食糧事情も若干良くなったとは言え、朝夕の食事は「お粥」と砂糖の入っていないミルクをバケツ一杯入れて飲み放題。夜中は空腹で眠られず、キャンプの広場に三々五々集まって来て内地の話などする。仰向になって空を仰ぐ、空には南十字星が神秘な瞬きをしている。東の空には、もうすぐ月が出るのか薄明るく見えた。
数時間後、月が出て来た。隣に寝ころがっていた見知らぬ兵が、
「来月の十五夜の月の出るまでには帰還の命令が来てくれないかなー」
と、つぶやいていた。
（本当になー。）

I heard General Yamashita was or had been in a separate barricade moving to the 1st camp. However, it didn't arouse any feelings in me.

Since I moved to the 6th Transport Unit, I had not seen my comrades in the 139th Logistics Hospital. I only saw Horiguchi when I was moving, so I was concerned about how they were.

The camp headquarters began to announce the returnees' list through a loudspeaker. Every Japanese soldier in the camp gathered in front of the headquarters at that time. They sat with their skinny knees in their arms, listening carefully and quietly. Those whose names were called looked as happy as could be. Those who weren't trudged back to their huts, shoulders drooping.

Though the food situation improved, rice porridge was still twice a day. However we could drink as much sugar-free milk as we wanted. We were too hungry to sleep at night. So we gathered in the open space of the camp in groups of twos and threes and talked about our hometowns in Japan. Lying on my back, I looked at the sky. The Southern Cross was blinking mystically. It was getting light in the east because the moon was about to rise.

A few hours later, the moon rose. A strange soldier lying beside me murmured, "I hope to get permission to return by the full moon next month."

How I wished I could!

12月もおしせまっていた時、例によって本部前に腰を下していた。「何の何太郎」と帰還者の氏名を次々と拡声器を通して呼出していた。

突然「浜辺政雄」と言う声が、私の耳に飛込む様に入って来ました。体の中を電気が流れたような頭の中を冷たい風が吹きぬけて行く様な感じです。浜辺政雄と呼ぶ声は突然と言えるような感じでした。その後、下着、洋服、靴、安全カミソリ、石けん等支給される。

いずれも夏服上衣にもズボンにもＰＷの文字をペンキ書きしていた。毛布一枚、安全カミソリで一年ぶりに髭をそる。栄養の加減か頭も髭もあまりのびていない様だ。靴をはいて歩けるようになっていた。

In late December, I sat in front of the headquarters as usual. They announced the returnees' names through the loudspeaker one after another.

Suddenly, I heard my name, "Masao Hamabe," called. I felt as if a cold wind blew through my head or an electric current had run through my body. The voice calling Masao Hamabe came as a sudden surprise. Later, I was supplied with underwear, clothes, shoes, safety razor, soap, etc. The letters P.W. were painted on summer jacket and pants. I shaved with safety razor and blanket for the first time in a year. Because of malnutrition, neither my hair nor beard had grown very much. I was able to walk in my US Army boots.

12　故国へ帰還

12 月 24 日、乗船のためキャンプを出発する。私物は一切持ち帰ってはならないと、きびしい告示あり。

小雨に煙るマニラ港と想われる。埠頭から船のタラップを登る。倉庫のような建物が並び、目の前は船で、附近の景色は全然見ることは出来なかった。船は米軍の御用船と言うか、上陸用舟艇でリバティ型とか。前の開かない船でダンブルの中の二重底に板を敷き、天幕を敷いてその上に皆ゴロ寝です。指揮者と言う人がなく、米兵は上の方におるだけで、一時ごたごたした。なんとか落着いたが立錐の余地もない。

12 月 24 日は「イブ」のため、船は出ない。翌日 25 日クリスマスで休み、26 日にやっと出港する。

ダンブルのハッチの上に木箱につめたレーションが山のように積んでいた。監視の米兵が 2 人銃を持って立っている。帰る船の中にいても食い物の事で頭が一杯。なんとかあのレーションを手に入れたいと思い、用もないのに梯子を昇ってデッキに出て見る。夜もやはり不寝番が立っていた。2、3 日運航すれど島影は見あたらない。

またデマが飛ぶ。

「我々を米本国につれていって去勢して一生ドレイとして使うそうだ」

そんな馬鹿な事があるものか、日が経つにつれ寒くなって来たので北に向かっていることは分かって安心した。

12 The return to my home country

On December 24, I left the camp to go aboard. We were strictly ordered not to bring our belongings.

Manila harbor looked dim in light rain. I walked up the gangway from the pier. Buildings like warehouses stood in a row, and a ship was in front. So I couldn't see the scenery.

The ship was called the Liberty type, the US wartime standard. The bow couldn't open. We put plates on the floor of a double bottom and spread tents so that we could lie. There was temporary confusion because of no leader, and the US soldiers on the upper deck didn't come. We settled somehow, but it was cramped.

No ships sailed on December 24 because it was Christmas Eve. The next day was the Christmas holiday.

On December 26, the ship left at last. The rations in crates were piled up on the upper deck. Two US soldiers stood watching with guns. I wanted to get rations somehow. Though I had nothing special to do, I climbed up the ladder to the deck. A US soldier stood on guard all night. We didn't see any islands for three days.

Someone spread a false rumor. "The boat will take us to the continental US to castrate and make us slaves for a lifetime."

It couldn't be such a foolish thing! It was getting colder as days passed, so I was relieved to know the ship was heading north.

ある夜、船のゆれがあまり激しいのに目をさます。暴風雨の中に突入したらしい。ひょっとしたらと思って梯子を昇ってデッキに出て見ると、ハッチの上に積んでいたレーションが下に落ち、木箱が割れ中身が飛び出していた。さっそく手に持てるだけ持って下におり、毛布を持って両隣の戦友を起こし、何回か往復する。当分満腹を味わう。

その日はとても寒い朝だったので、皆早くから起きていた。

デッキ監視の米兵が「フジヤマ、フジヤマ」と叫んで飛び回っているので、皆梯子にむれ集まり、我先にとデッキに出る。私もデッキに出て見たら、富士山は1月初旬で真っ白に雪を頂き荘厳な姿を見せて我々を見守ってくれている様だった。

見ている内に涙が後から後から流れ出た。隣の戦友もまた隣も数百名の人間が皆涙を流し、ふきもせず富士の姿を凝視し続けた。

ふと気が付くと、船の近くを小さな漁船がいて3人ほどの人が乗っていた。「縄ハイ」と言う漁法で鯛を獲っていたようで、立ち上がって鯛を両手でかかえ上げ、上下させていた。無事に帰って来られておめでとうと言っているようでした。

皆も気がついて、「万歳、万歳」とさけんで泣いていた。

One night, the ship's violent roll woke me up. Seemingly, we were involved in a storm. "Maybe?" It occurred to me that this storm had brought something good. I climbed up the ladder and onto the deck. The rations had fallen. Some crates were cracked, and the contents had popped out. I brought back as many rations as I could. I woke up my fellow soldiers on both sides. Then we went back and forth several times with blankets. We had enough for several days.

It was a freezing morning, so everyone was up early. Some US soldiers watching on the deck were running about, shouting, "Fujiyama, Fujiyama!" We gathered around the ladder and scrambled up to the deck.

When I reached the deck, I could see Mt. Fuji covered with snow in early January. Showing her magnificent shape, Mt. Fuji seemed to be watching over us. While looking at Mt. Fuji, I shed tears continuously. Fellow soldiers beside and around me shed tears. Hundreds of Japanese soldiers on the ship did too. Not wiping tears, we kept gazing at Mt. Fuji.

I suddenly noticed a small fishing boat with three men near our ship. They seemed to be catching sea breams. One of them stood up with a sea bream in his hands, raising and lowering it. He seemed to say, "Congratulations for coming back safe and sound! "

Everyone on our ship noticed him and was shouting with tears, "Banzai! Banzai!"

* A sea bream symbolizes a happy event in Japan, which means "auspicious". *

神奈川県浦賀港に入港、「ハシケ」に乗りかえ上陸し、宿舎の連隊に向かう。昭和21年の新春の松の内なので日本髪の娘さん達もちらほら見えた。

復員手続きを終え、山で未払だった俸給として120円あまりもらった。わあ一大金だ。

1日外出が出来た。銭湯の券をもらって風呂に入る。

浦賀駅前広場で戸板に乗せて「みかん」を5個くらい、一山にして売っている。私達は出征前の感覚で一山10銭と読んだ、と言うよりそう思い込んで、

「ハアみかんだ。日本の果物だ」と言う事でバーッと並ぶ。自分の巡番のくるのが待ち遠しいと思いながら見ていると、皆みかんを買わずにすごすご立ち去る。良く見たら「一山10円」と書いてあった。びっくりした。

1月11日、浦賀より長崎に向かって帰る。

汽車は門司港乗り替えで1時間あまり長崎行に間があった。長崎は原子爆弾で全滅と聞いていたし、また山の中で敵のビラを見たこともあり、鹿児島の叔母の家にと思ったが、長崎に帰った。

家も両親も弟妹も皆無事だった。

家に帰りついて、1時間ほどしたら眠気が出て2日ばかり眠り続けた。

The ship entered Uraga Port in Kanagawa Prefecture. We boarded a barge and went ashore to the regiment's quarters. It was New Year's Week in 1946. There were some young girls in Nihongami, the traditional Japanese hairstyle for women. I finished the demobilization procedure. I received over 120 yen as my military salary, which had not been paid in the Philippines.

"Wow, that's a lot of money."

We could go out for a day. I had a good time taking a bath with a public bath ticket.

They were selling five mandarin oranges in a pile on a board at a stall in Uraga Station Square. "Wow! Mandarin, Japanese fruit." We stood in line, assuming we could buy them for ten sen from the pre-war value of money. I could hardly wait for my turn. However, everyone before me walked away dejectedly without buying one. I looked well and found it was written "10 yen a pile". I was surprised at the price.

*(The value of money had changed.)

On January 11, I left Uraga for Nagasaki. I changed trains at Moji-port station. There was more than an hour before the train for Nagasaki. I heard an atomic bomb had destroyed Nagasaki, and I had seen enemy leaflets in the mountains. So I thought I should go to my aunt's house in Kagoshima, but I returned to Nagasaki.

My house, parents, and younger brothers and sisters were all safe. An hour after I got home, I became sleepy and slept continuously for two days.

著者独白（昭和六十一年新春）

無事復員出来たのも、病気がちな私が条件の悪い山中で病気をしなかった、と言う事も、戦友達や先祖の「みたま」のおかげと今も感謝しています。

私の長女が熊本の人と結婚して浦賀の浦賀台と言う所に住んでいましたので、二年ほど前、家内と二人遊びに行きました。復員した時、入港した港、日本鋼管の造船所の門を左に見ながら歩いたような記憶がありました。しかし駅前広場も復員手続きをした宿舎の連隊跡も分かりませんでした。今度行った時は役所に聞いて見ようと思っています。

在天の戦友達の霊に心よりの御冥福を祈ります。

（おわり）

Epilogue January 1986

I did not get sick in bad conditions in the mountains and was able to be demobilized. I am grateful and owe all to the spirit of my ancestors and departed war comrades.

Two years ago, my wife and I went to Uraga, where my eldest daughter lived with her husband from Kumamoto.

I remembered walking by the gate of the Nihon-Koukan shipyard on my left at the port when I was demobilized. However, I didn't recognize the station square or trace of regiment's quarters where I got demobilization procedure. I will ask the government office next time I go to Uraga.

From the bottom of my heart, I pray the souls of my comrades rest in peace in heaven.

(Fin)

第139兵站病院の戦友会 昭和45年4月18日

前から2列目の中腰の人の左から5人目が筆者。右上枠内は、部隊長の山田健 軍医少佐。九州出身者が多い総勢450人の部隊であった。(日赤から派遣の看護婦の方は含めず) 同年兵119人中戦死者は64人 (戦死率54%)

当時フィリピン全島の日本人(軍人と在留邦人) 65万人のうち、戦争直後10万人。その半数が栄養失調や疾病で死亡し、日本へ帰還できた者は5万人と言われる。ちなみにレイテ島に派遣された第138兵站病院は、ほぼ全滅。

生い立ち

大正11年2月8日長崎県西彼杵郡小ヶ倉村(現 長崎市小ヶ倉町)にて出生。
小学1年の2学期より樺太の恵須取に一家で移り住む
恵須取小学校高等科を卒業した後、一家は長崎に帰郷
徴兵されるまでは、東京で仕事をしていました。
戦後は、昭和24年に結婚。生活の苦しい昭和20年代を経て、昭和31年から長崎三菱造船所に勤務していました。
平成2年7月29日午後7時29分逝去　享年68 (肺癌にて)

A reunion of comrades at the 139th Logistics Hospital April 18, 1970

From the front, Masao Hamabe is fifth from the left in the second row, crouching.The person framed in the right corner is Major Takeshi Yamada, an army surgeon and commanding officer. It was a unit of 450 people; many were from Kyushu, excluding the nurses dispatched by the Japanese Red Cross Society. There were 119 recruits, 64 were killed in the war (54% death rate).

At the time, 650,000 Japanese, both soldiers and residents, lived in the Philippines. When the war ended, 100,000 survived. However, half of the survivors died of malnutrition or diseases, and it is said 50,000 people returned to Japan.

Nearly all 138th Logistics Hospital soldiers dispatched to Leyte Island were killed.

Masao Hamabe's Personal History

On February 8, 1922, he was born in Kogakura village, Nagasaki Prefecture. (In those days, Kogakura wasn't part of Nagasaki city.)

He and his family moved to Estori town in Karafuto, in his second term of first grade in elementary school. The town is now called Uglegorsk by Russians. They had to move because his grandfather, Umetaro Hamabe (1878-1935), had gone out of business. Mr. Taketugu, his mother's father, objected to Masao and his mother Miya going to Karafuto, but he died next year.

After he graduated from Estori Higher Elementary School, the family returned to Nagasaki.

Masao worked in Tokyo until he was drafted into the army. After the war, he married in 1949 and worked at the Nagasaki Mitsubishi Shipyard from 1956.

He died of lung cancer at 7:29 p.m. on July 29, 1990, when he was 68.

あとがき

父、濱辺政雄は、衛生兵としてルソン島の比島派遣第139兵站病院という部隊に所属しておりました。

戦後、部隊の戦友会で各人の体験記を集めて「比島おもいで集」と題した文集が作られました。一つは昭和49年、もう一つは昭和61年です。

その2編を時系列的に一つにまとめ、雑誌「丸」の2019年4月号と5月号に掲載されました。父の原稿は、できる限り変更しておりません。

読みやすいように、章立てのみは、私が書き加えております。

より多くの人に読んでいただきたく、今回、英訳し、父の日本語の文と英訳を一つの本にいたしました。

英訳の際の御助言を、長崎在住のデニス・ウィルキンソン氏にいただいたこと、感謝しております。

濱辺淳一

遥かフィリピンの戦没者を偲ぶ著者（昭和40年頃）

Masao Hamabe around 1965

He is thinking of his fellow soldiers who died in the Philippines.

During World War II, my father, Masao Hamabe, was a medic at the 139th Logistics Hospital on Luzon Island, the Philippines.

After the war, the 139th corps reunion produced two collections of each soldier's experience, in 1974 and in 1986.

My father's two notes were edited in time order and published in April and May 2019 issues of the magazine "Maru". I have hardly changed my father's original manuscript. I have added only the headings for each chapter so that readers can understand the content more quickly.

Hoping more people would read it, I translated it into English and published the Japanese draft and translated text in one volume.

I am grateful to Mr. Dennis Wilkinson, who lives in Nagasaki, for his advice on the English translation.

Junichi Hamabe

陸軍衛生二等兵
ルソン島生還記

発行日	初版2023年（令和5）2月8日
著　者	濱辺政雄
発行人	片山仁志
編集人	川良真理
発行所	株式会社長崎文献社 〒850-0057 長崎市大黒町3-1　長崎交通産業ビル5階 TEL.095-823-5247　FAX.095-823-5252 メール　info@e-bunken.com　nagasakibunkensha@gmail.com ホームページ　http://www.e-bunken.com
印　刷	株式会社インテックス

ISBN978-4-88851-381-4　C0095

◇定価はカバーに表示してあります。
◇落丁本、乱丁本は発行元にお送りください。送料当方負担でお取り換えします。